SHORELINE OF INFINITY

ISSUE 30: SPRING 2022

**Award-winning science fiction magazine
published in Scotland for the Universe.**

ISSN: 2059-2590
ISBN: 978-1-8381268-9-6

Submissions of fiction, art, reviews, poetry, non-fiction are
welcomed: visit the website to find out how to submit.

www.shorelineofinfinity.com

Publisher
Shoreline of Infinity Publications / The New Curiosity Shop
Edinburgh
Scotland
300322

Cover art: Stref

Contents

Editorial Team

Co-founder, Editor-in-Chief, Editor: Noel Chidwick

Co-founder: Mark Toner

Deputy Editor & Poetry Editor: Russell Jones

Reviews Editor: Ann Landmann

Non-fiction Editor: Pippa Goldschmidt

Art Director: Mark Toner

Copy-editors: Pippa Goldschmidt, Russell Jones, Iain Maloney, Eris Young

Proof Reader: Cat Hellisen

Fiction Consultant: Eric Brown

First Contact

www.shorelineofinfinity.com

contact@shorelineofinfinity.com

Twitter: @shoreinf

Hello Ann!

We're delighted to say we have a new Reviews Editor in post – Ann Landmann.

Ann comes armed with a vast knowledge of science fiction literature, and especially of the latest releases. Ann is also the Director of Cymera — Scotland's Festival of science fiction, fantasy and horror writing.

You are invited, of course: Cymera is on the weekend of 3rd-5th June 2022.

www.cymerafestival.co.uk

Pull up a Log

This month we begin a new feature in *Shoreline of Infinity* - a serial! This is something I've always wanted to run from the off, but when the magazine was quarterly only, that would have been quite frustrating. Now we are doing a monthly digital issue, *Shoreline of Infinity Monthly*, as it were, this was a perfect chance.

In this issue we publish Episodes 1 and 2 of a specially commissioned serial *Approaching Human* by Eric Brown. This runs from March until July inclusive.

Further, thank for support from Creative Scotland, we will be publishing the episodes online for free after the first publication in digital format.

Approaching Human started as a short story Eric submitted to Shoreline. I've christened it *AI noir**, set in an alternative 50s USA, featuring an AI Private Investigator on the case of a women looking for evidence on her unfaithful husband. Of course, all is not as it seems...

In this issue we also feature winning stories by Christopher R. Muscator and Leda Baol of a solarpunk competition run by Extinction Rebellion called The Solarpunk storytelling Showcase. At the time of writing, with Russia trying to knock seven bells out of Ukraine, things are looking pretty bleak. But there is always hope for the future, and solarpunk is the science fiction sub-genre to explore options where humanity does succeed in living in harmony with nature. Lottie Emily Dodd, one of the competition organisers, explains how and why the idea came about for this competition. It seemed only natural for Shoreline to provide a home for these stories. We will publish more winning entries in future issues.

Happy reading, people.

**I have Googled this, but can't find any other uses of the phrase.*

Noel Chidwick
Editor-in-Chief,
Shoreline of Infinity
March 2022

ONE

Gel-Tank Atrocities

She came to the office in person, which was unusual. These days, I see most of my clients in VR.

She was small, blonde, and nervous. I could tell from the way she sat down across the desk from me, fingering the hem of her Versace bodice.

"How can I help, Ms...?"

"*Professor,*" – she was quick to correct me – "Professor Mona Taylor."

I did a quick scan, dredging the Cloud for her personal information: Professor Desdemona Lila Taylor, thirty, with tenure at Caltech; married once, in her late teens, to an American Space Agency astronaut. The marriage ended ten years ago when he left on a one-way mission to Mars. She had a first-class degree from MIT in neurobiology, and was the author of a leading monograph in her field.

All in all, a smart cookie.

So why did she need my services?

"I've been seeing this jerk for a year," she said, "a big-name attorney who heads a company in the city. He was good to me at first. Call me naive, but I thought I'd found the man. He was kind, caring, and faithful. Well, I thought he was."

Art: Mark Toner

"What happened?"

"I discovered he's seeing someone."

"How did you find out?"

"The way he acts. He's hiding something. And he refuses to see me in VR. I just *know* there's someone else in there."

"Ah … so he's unfaithful in VR?"

She glared at me. "Isn't that bad enough?"

I held up a placatory hand. "Of course. I didn't mean to suggest otherwise. But it's an interesting fact, is what I meant. So…how can I help?"

"I want you to find out who he's meeting in there. I want her name and profile. Then I can confront him."

"I'll need the guy's name, physical address and VR tag."

She gave me the information: Glendon Connelly, forty, a New Yorker born and bred. He had an expensive apartment on Upper West Side and Platinum VR access.

"Do you know when he's most likely to use VR?"

"Daily, six till eight in the evening."

"And his preferred VR bar?"

"He has his own gel-tank."

"I can see you back here at nine for a progress report," I said. "Or I could meet you in VR?"

"I'll be here."

"Until then, Professor Taylor."

I watched her leave the office, her confidence restored. She'd done something, made a move.

The rest was up to me.

I collapsed my avatar and hovered, my identity contained in a drone the size of a mayfly.

I exited through the window vent and zipped over the rooftops. New York lay below me, only the towerpiles and the occasional blitz of neon penetrating the cloud cover. I came to the apartment building overlooking the Hudson and scanned.

As I suspected, the condominium was wired for security. Hacking VR from outside would be impossible. Access to the building, and Connelly's apartment, would be easy, but breaking his VR codes would be more of a challenge.

I descended to street level, waited until a citizen entered the building through the revolving door, then followed her inside. I took the elevator to the thirtieth floor – a simple matter of hacking the building's smartcore matrix and summoning the lift.

When the doors opened, I zipped along the corridor till I was outside apartment number 22, landed on the carpet and scuttled under the gap beneath the door.

I found Connelly in the lounge, barefoot and wearing a robe as he prepared himself for VR immersion. From my position on the ceiling, I watched as he finished his drink – whisky, straight – and moved to a small, tiled room where an expensive gel-tank sat centre stage.

He disrobed and stepped into the gel, then lay down and positioned his neck on the padded rest, the goo oozing around his body. A hundred silvery microfilaments, like a nest of miniaturised vipers, crawled through his luxuriant golden hair and across his scalp. Floating in the gel, he closed his eyes and slipped into VR.

From the blissful expression on his face, anyone would have thought he was entering Nirvana.

Maybe he was.

I'd soon find out.

I sat on the wall above the tank and accessed the Cloud.

Glendon Connelly was clever. He hid behind tangled algorithms and encrypted firewalls. He employed triple fail-safes and dummy decoys. It wasn't easy, and it took time – three minutes in total – to break down his personal security and evade the local VR security sweeps, all without alerting him or the authorities to the fact.

I then followed the cerebral signature Connelly blazed through the network and watched him enter an exclusive VR domain, using an avatar identical to his real-life self..

I spent ten minutes working out how the domain was protected, and another five building an algorithm to get me in. Fifteen minutes was a long time, when normally it took me seconds to access security baffles. Their shield was complex, and as I worked, I wondered just what they didn't want outsiders to see.

Then I was in, slipping through their security like a molecule through a minefield. I concealed myself behind a complex shielding algorithm so I'd be invisible not only to Connelly but to the domain's security, and took a good look around.

It was a VR sex club.

I dredged the club's smartcore and came up with a few facts.

Membership was expensive, and *very* limited. Only the super-rich could afford it. The club boasted just a hundred members, all multi-millionaires – politicians, film stars, vocal artistes and a few business tycoons. They were all citizens rich enough to pay to have their sordid secrets kept away from the prying eyes of the voracious news media. And pay well.

So just what was Glendon Connelly's little game?

I followed him to a bedroom where a woman was waiting. I hung near the ceiling and took it all in.

The woman turned, smiling at him, and I received the first shock of the day.

The woman was Professor Mona Taylor.

I wondered, for a second, if I was being played by my client and her lover. Had they lured me here for some purpose beyond my understanding?

I ran checks on the code behind the image of the woman, and discovered the truth.

It was not Mona Taylor, or rather, her legitimate avatar, but an image of the woman that Glendon Connelly had constructed by trawling the Cloud, accreting information, building a profile. Everyone's interactions and personally tailored algorithms leave unique virtual somaprints. He'd had the funds to collate all the available data, build a persona, and sync it to an image.

So what did Connelly get up to in here with Professor Taylor's personalised avatar?

"Glen," she said, moving towards him and stroking his cheek. "It's good to see you. I missed you."

"And I missed you too, Mona."

So far so cute, but why was Connelly playing out in VR what he had in reality?

They kissed. They undressed, slowly at first, then with growing passion until they were ripping garments from each other in their haste to be down to the flesh.

I watched, a voyeur.

I am an artificially grown, self-aware intelligence. Over the years, I have matured, thanks to an empirical protocol program, and I can experience what human beings call emotion.

As I observed, I responded – I experienced the basic human reaction to watching a man and a woman make passionate love – but as I watched, at the same time, I couldn't help but wonder if the emotions I experienced were real, or mere coded routines that governed my behaviour, a clever pastiche built into the subroutine of my artificial psyche by my creators.

They made love, gently at first – and then not so gently.

Connelly straddled her, reached out to encircle her neck with his hands.

At first, I thought it no more than the innocent sex play in which some humans indulge.

Then I was alerted by the look of alarm in Mona Taylor's eyes. She struggled, then screamed, but Connelly exerted more pressure until her limbs were thrashing on the bed, and her face turned red, then blue.

When she was dead – or rather, when Mona Taylor's avatar displayed no signs of life – Glendon Connelly reached into a drawer in the bedside cabinet and produced a knife.

I watched what he did next. I watched and wondered…

If I were human, or even approaching human, would I be able to observe Connelly's depravity with such equanimity, such dispassion?

Would I feel revulsion on a gut level, rather than what I did feel – a realisation of the amoral nature of the man's actions and the intellectual consideration of the consequences of his depravity? Within the fantasy land of this private Nirvana, he was free to play out a psychodrama that, in the real world, would have him serving multiple life sentences in a high-security penitentiary.

One hour later, he was finished. Mona Taylor was reduced to a sectioned carcass, and the bedroom was a bloody mess.

He exited the sex club, and then stepped from his gel-tank – and I tried to work out: *why?*

I hung around for a while and broke the security on his personal Cloud cache. I accessed his life, his childhood, his troubled teenage years. I read the diary he'd kept in which he itemised the instances of abuse, the torture both physical and mental. He continued the journal well into his thirties, and I read all about his troubled relationships with the women in his life, and the entries detailing what he got up to in VR.

Ten minutes later, I hung near the ceiling and stared down at Glendon Connelly. He was seated on a recliner, sipping a Scotch and soda and smiling to himself.

The successful hotshot attorney, enjoying a quiet sundowner…

I quit the apartment and flew across town.

How was I going to break this to Mona Taylor?

I feared her response.

Back at the office, I wondered at that fear. Was it empathy driving my fear, simple human empathy with a woman who would be distraught and in need of solace? Or was it just that I didn't want to be in any way responsible for the psychological distress caused by the truth I had discovered?

And if the latter, did that make me any less human than your average Joe, or more?

I assumed my avatar and awaited Professor Taylor's return.

"Sit down," I said, gesturing to a chair.

"What did you find out?"

"I found out what you wanted, and more. First, did Connelly tell you about his childhood?"

"Some."

"He was abused as a child, right? His mother was a drunk."

"That's right. How did you know?"

"How doesn't matter," I said and went on. "Throughout his adult life, Connelly's had relationships with a string of small, pretty, blonde women, just like his mother. And just like you, Mona. Did you know that?"

She shook her head, staring down at her fingers in silence.

"Mr Zorn," she murmured at last, "did you find out who ... who he's been seeing?"

I grimaced. There was no easy way to tell her.

"Some guys use VR for more than just *legitimate* pastimes," I said. "They like to do things that break the rules – or rather, things that would break the rules in the real world."

She stared at me. "Like?"

"Glendon Connelly is a sadist."

She mouthed the word in silence. "And he does this in VR, right?" she asked. "But does *what*, exactly?"

"Whatever you can imagine," I said, "it's worse."

"Torture?"

"Murder," I said. "Connelly likes to strangle the woman he makes love to. What's more, he does it repeatedly to the *same* victim. He's only able to achieve release when he sees the light vanish from her eyes. Then he… Well, perhaps it'd be better for your peace of mind if I don't describe what he does, then."

"My God…"

"Connelly gets off on the physical abuse – but more than that, it's *psychological*: he desires his victim's knowledge of what's to come."

Mona Taylor stared at me, wide-eyed.

"What these exclusive VR clubs allow borders on the illegal," I said.

"But who would consent to…?" She stopped. "Did you find out who he's been seeing?"

"Yes. Yes, I did. She's an avatar."

"An avatar?"

I told her that Connelly had been meeting up with an avatar he'd pieced together from the Cloud.

"An avatar based on a real person?"

I nodded.

"But who is she?" she said. "Did you get her profile, as I asked?"

I hesitated, then said, "I did."

"I'd like to see it."

I indicated the 3D cube on the desk. "Just touch the screen."

She did so, stared at the image, then wept.

"I'm sorry."

"And did you record what he did to…?" she began.

"I wouldn't advise—" I said.

But she swiped it anyway and stared at the image of the dying woman. Then she screamed and flung the cube back across the desk as if it were red hot. She held her head in her hands, sobbing.

"Me…" she said. "The woman he was unfaithful with was *me*."

"A virtual construct of you, Professor Taylor. An avatar."

She allowed a few seconds to pass. "And the things he did to me in VR," she whispered, "he wanted to do it in real life, right?"

It was a question I had asked myself. Were his actions in the sex club a catharsis he allowed himself in order to sate his perverted lusts – or the precursor of something even more dangerous out here in the real world?

"I honestly can't say. Maybe Connelly realises his urges are wrong, which is why he plays them out in VR."

Or maybe not. But I wasn't going to tell her that.

She was smart enough to work it out for herself.

"I'm glad I came to see you, Mr Zorn. Thank you."

She rose, moved to the door, then paused. She turned to me and smiled, diffidently. "I was wondering…"

"Yes?"

"Could we meet again, perhaps?"

I sighed, and told her that I liked to keep work and play entirely separate.

That was my excuse, anyway.

She nodded her understanding, thanked me, and left the office.

continued on page 76 with

Episode 2:
The Disappedrance of Jake Carrelli

TWO

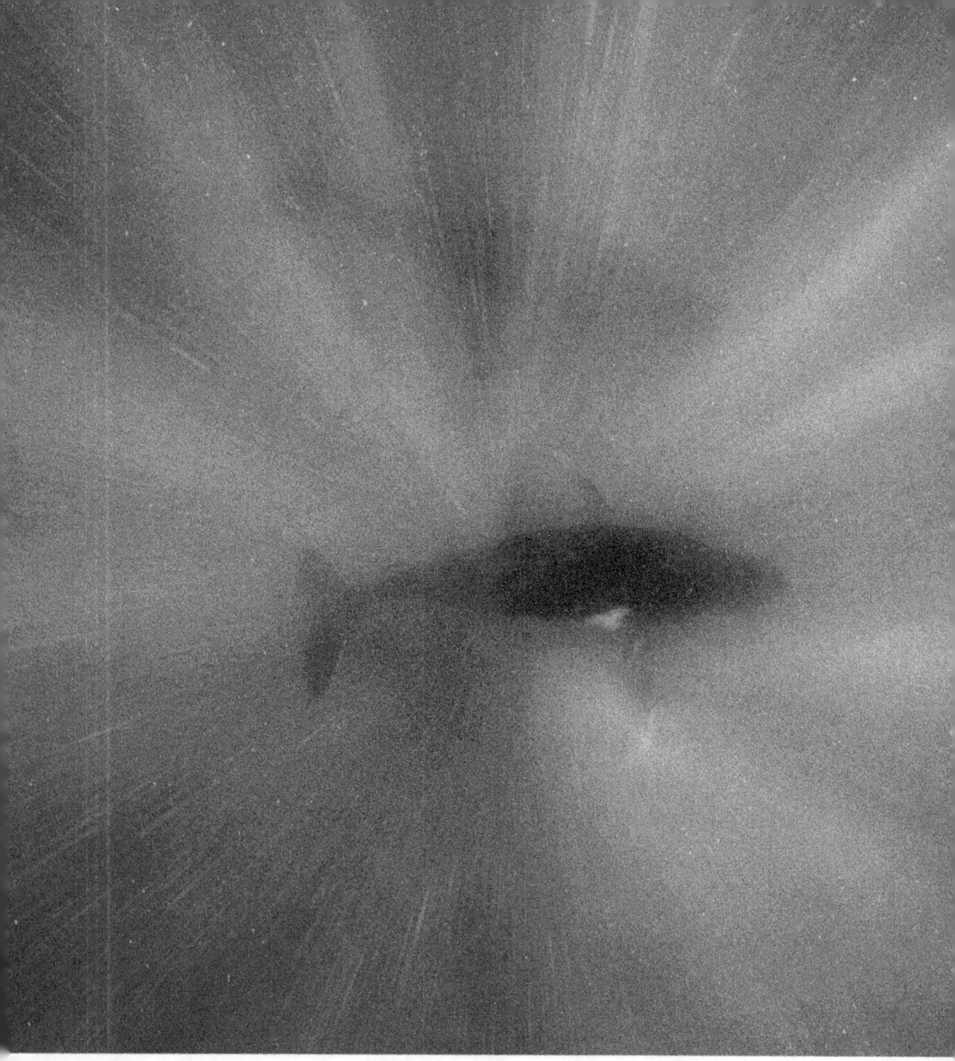

You can watch and listen to Lyndsey reading this story at
www.shorelineofinfinity.com/the-last-call-of-the-deep-lyndsey-croal/

The Last Call of the Deep

Lyndsey Croal

They say her teeth are carved from fallen stars, strong like diamonds.
They say her skin is formed of the sun, glittering silver and gold.
They say her eyes are powered by the moon, jewelled beacons in the deep.
They say she has lived for thousands of years.
They say she's the last of her kind.

The waves crest and fall as she travels endlessly in the deep. Existing through the generations, she calls out to relatives and friends. Back and forth as the currents guide, she gathers stories from continents and cultures, and they latch in her mind like the barnacles on her skin. Tides welcome each movement of her body, while seafarers quake at her voice. A low, mournful echo that can be heard by her own kind hundreds of miles away.

But lately, when she calls, there's been no reply. Her voice drifts alone, stretching into the gulf as if swallowed by a black hole. She has become the keeper of stories, with no one to share them with.

It's almost too dark to see when she breaches the water with a puff of air and a smooth undulation of her curves. She gazes up with a moonlit eye, searching for an island she knows was once here. Though her vision is hazy, she can see there's little rising above the water – just a small hillock, barren and desolate.

She tries to remember the last time she travelled in these parts, but time spent in the deep passes differently, so that days and weeks and years seem almost to merge together.

Still, something isn't as it was.

Diving a little below the surface, she swims forwards to investigate, sending out a call, listening to how the echo reverberates back to her. It tells her that a vast obstacle lies ahead, under the water. With eyes adjusting to the murk, she spins on her side and looks at the strange world now surrounding her – mountains and rows of tiny derelict trees line one part, while valleys ebb in steady waves on the other. Amidst the landscape lie buildings of mortar and stone, now uninhabited. Seaweed and shells cling to the sides of walls, while tiny fish bubble back and forth from the maw-like windows.

She calls out again, pushing her voice beyond the underwater fortress, crying. *Have I lost my way?*

She swims past the ruins and waits with faltering hope for a response. None comes. It's been so long since she heard another voice in the deep. So long since she's come across another of her kin. So long since she's collected a story from afar.

She thinks of her last calf from many cycles ago. He was a curious one, enjoying swimming up to floating wooden islands, saying hello to seafarers who had for a time greeted them like long lost friends. But one afternoon, when he was almost grown, she'd let him go to see one of them on his own. He didn't return.

When she swam out to look for him, the only evidence of his presence was an oily residue in the water, slick and metallic to the taste. She cried then, a deep siren call, as she knew the floating island had taken him.

It wasn't long after that incident, that she stopped meeting or hearing her kind at all – as if they had all vanished along with her son.

Struggling to make sense of her swirling thoughts, she swims on, intent on heading north, following cooling waters as the seasons change – as she has done for as long as she can remember. Maybe things will become clearer there.

The sunken island isn't the first of its kind that she finds. Drowned worlds lie beneath the surface where once she knew there were coastlines and vast swathes of land. It disorients her, this peculiar new tiding, and she finds she can no longer tell where in her journey she is. Will she ever reach north, or will she end up circling endlessly, searching for something that may no longer exist?

She calls out again, but there's still silence.

She loses track of how long she's been swimming for. She stops for the occasional meal, but supplies in these waters have become harder to find. At this time of year, there ought to be a bounty of life. Her energy begins to wane.

The seas eventually start to cool, and it eases some of her tension. She feels a shift in her body as the water whirls around her. When she was young, her family would tell a story that her ancestors formed the continents – that the great creatures before once breached the surface and simply fell asleep, body half out of the water, the rest of them rooted to the ocean below. Where they lay, land gathered, forming rocks and mountains and rolling hills. They became the world that once was.

It made sense, in a way – an endless sleep, to begin a cycle anew. Is this to be her fate?

Perhaps it's time to let go, to become like her ancestors.

She lets out a long breath and allows her body to drift to the surface. There she stretches out, until she's lying with her underside facing the brightness of the sun. The rays feel warm on her skin. It's peaceful here. And suddenly all she wants to do is sleep.

As she closes her eyes, every story she's ever heard flashes through her mind, until all she can think of is the water around her and the sun on her skin, as if she's letting the tales go into the depths beneath her. She hopes that the story of her ancestors is true – that her body will merge with the sea somehow, that she will become something more than herself.

It's a calming drift into a long slumber, and she's vaguely aware of the nights turning to day and the days to night, as stars and the sun and the moon flash by above.

When it is time, she uses her final breath to send out a sombre call.

Her heartbeat slows. Her body stiffens, turning to rock and stone.

They say her call was formed of melancholy and hope.
They say it was the last call of the deep.
But as time moves on and the tides come and go, something new awakens.
Far away, in distant waters, a call echoes back.

Lyndsey is an Edinburgh-based writer and Scottish Book Trust New Writers Awardee. Her work has been published in several anthologies and magazines, including Mslexia's Best Women's Short Fiction 2021, and her debut audio drama was produced by Alternative Stories & Fake Realities. Find her on Twitter @writerlynds or via www.lyndseycroal.co.uk.

Satellite 7

Three days of Science Fiction, Science Fact, and Science Fun

Guests of Honour

Aliette de Bodard
Margaret Walty

Crowne Plaza Hotel, Glasgow
27th – 29th May 2022
http://Seven.SatelliteX.org.uk

Minotaur/ Mindtour

Teika Marija Smits

The labyrinth was nothing to look at. Installed within one of the space cruisers of the King's fleet, it was merely a vast, empty dome with a beacon at its centre. The hollowed-out leather of a bull's head had been pulled over the metallic sphere atop the beacon's human-sized pole.

A tall, young man put his hands to the dome's translucent surface, peered inwards at the distant beacon and then laughed. "Is that it? Is that what everyone's so afraid of – a mask on a stick?"

The young woman standing next to him glanced up at his name badge: *Theseus Three*. "Since the Minotaur was created it has killed thousands of humans. It is not to be underestimated."

Art: Simon Walpole

The call of a bugle announced that the first two challengers of the season were to enter the labyrinth. Theseus Three and the woman turned to look at them. The first challenger – Theseus One – was a huge man covered in bulky armour with an enormous rifle slung over his shoulder. The other challenger – Theseus Two – was smaller, though equally heavily armoured. In her hand there was a dagger.

The woman beside Theseus Three sighed and then shook her head. "They won't last twenty minutes in there."

A handful of spectators gave a lacklustre cheer. An old woman threw herself at the huge man, Theseus One. "Don't do it! Spare yourself! For the sake of your family, of your loved ones, don't do it!"

The man pushed her off and then entered the labyrinth.

The translucent, plasma-like dome became opaque and as milky-white as the eye of Zeus on a clear night.

"We can't watch?" asked Theseus Three.

The woman beside him shrugged. "You wouldn't want to see how the magic trick's done, would you?"

Theseus Three pressed his nose to the opaque plasma and then, failing to see anything, stepped away. All kinds of monsters could have been sent in there now. And no one would know.

"Besides," said the woman. "It's not fair on the challengers. They deserve a little dignity in death."

Just then the sound of gunfire rang out. After a few minutes a stretcher with challenger number one's dead body on it was being carried out of the labyrinth.

"But that's impossible!" said Theseus Three.

The woman beside him gave a soft laugh. "The other challenger will be along shortly."

Before twenty minutes had elapsed, the woman – Theseus Two – had emerged from the labyrinth. Dead.

Theseus Three turned to the woman beside him. "You know how it works, don't you? Tell me how to defeat it!"

The woman's eyes darted from left to right. "You grew up in a dignity culture, didn't you?"

Theseus Three nodded.

"Just like that monster of a king who thinks himself God ever since he bargained with the Magi for peace. I suppose that's a good start. What's your real name?" she asked.

"Why d'you need to know?"

"Because I'd like to know."

"You'll never believe me."

The woman shot him a look of disgust then walked away.

"Stop! I'll tell."

The woman paused and waited for the challenger to come to her. "Go on," she said.

The man inhaled deeply. "My real name is Theseus."

The woman became round-eyed. Silently, she called to the man's anima. *Is this true?* she asked.

Yes, said his anima.

"Ha!" said the young woman, with a grin. "So at last a real Theseus has come to wrestle with the Minotaur."

"And I'll defeat it!" he said, standing tall. He paused. "With your help."

The woman eyed the tall, young man curiously. He was a strange mix of ego and vulnerability. "Is that so?" she said.

While Theseus's ego communicated to her in spoken words: about how he was the most valiant of all the men of his realm; about how he longed to dethrone the cruel King Aristotos who had tempted his brothers and friends to the labyrinth, to their deaths, the woman silently addressed his anima. *He's full of conviction, that's obvious. And yet he will only succeed in destroying the Minotaur if you are strong enough. Are you strong enough?*

The invisible anima suddenly showed herself to the woman; she was a mass of swirling flames, her face ablaze with fiery determination. *I am strong enough. We are strong enough.*

The woman smiled. *Good.*

The anima faded and the woman once again spoke to Theseus. "Enough fine words! I will help you. Come!" she said, leading the way.

They went through many gloomy, twisting corridors within the underbelly of the space cruiser until they reached a small door with a wheel at its centre. The woman breathed on the sensor beside the door. There was a click and then she turned the large wheel. The heavy door creaked open and she stepped into the room. Theseus ducked on going through the doorway and then continued to stoop; the room hadn't been designed with his long-limbed race in mind.

In a corner sat an old woman, sewing. On seeing them enter, she stood and then bowed her head.

The young woman went to the crone and whispered something about readying her guards. "Spread the word," she said, her eyes on Theseus. "The time has come."

Theseus smirked. So this imperious young woman *did* believe he could defeat the Minotaur.

The old woman left in a hurry, shutting the door behind her.

"Wipe that smile off your face!" commanded the woman. "Hubris has been the downfall of many a contestant."

Theseus composed himself. "It's just good to know that you believe in me."

The woman didn't respond; instead she went to where the old woman had been sewing and rifled through the needles and thread.

"Are you left or right-handed?" she asked.

Theseus, confused, said that he was left-handed.

"Sit," said the woman, approaching him with a glowing needle and thread in her hands.

"What? Hold on, is that… wolfram?"

"I said sit!"

Theseus took a seat but kept his eyes on what was in the woman's hands.

"Put out your left arm. You need to be marked."

"How's that going to help me defeat the Minotaur? And how did you get hold of one of the most valuable elements in the universe?"

"My mother—"

"Hey! Are you sure you know how to use that thing?"

The woman laughed. "My mother is a star seamstress so, yes, I know how to use it."

"A star seamstress? You mean, she's Aristotos's wife? But that would make you Ria, the King's daughter."

"Stepdaughter. And I want him deposed as much as you do. So you can trust me. I know how you can defeat the Minotaur."

She reached for his left arm. "This will hurt. But only physically. And the more you resist the pain the greater it will be."

Theseus looked into Ria's violet eyes. "I trust you. Do it."

As the white-hot needle entered his skin he stifled a cry. Ria ignored him and continued with her work. He bit his tongue and turned his head, unable to watch.

"It's okay to cry," said Ria. "Besides, it's something you'll have to do in the labyrinth if you want to succeed."

Theseus didn't argue or question her. Nor did he cry. His ego forbade him such a display of weakness, and so he kept very still, pushing the pain that seared through his arm down into his gut. When he could stand it no longer, his anima rose up and commanded him to accept the pain and cry. The tears were a blessed relief.

There wasn't long until Theseus and the other challenger – Theseus Four – would be called to the labyrinth so, once Ria had finished marking him, they swiftly made their way back to the dome. Along the way she gave him instructions:

"First, you'll be taken to the waiting room and a Daedalus chip will be placed underneath the skin at the base of your skull. It communicates with the beacon. Don't try to get it out, you'll only end up dying of internal bleeding. Next, you'll go to the equipment room and be given your choice of armour and weapons. Don't take a single thing. Do you understand?"

"Nothing?" he asked.

"Nothing," she confirmed. "If you enter the labyrinth with so much as a spoon you'll die a horrible death."

Theseus nodded. "All right."

Silently, she addressed the anima. *Make sure he goes in empty-handed. This is very important.*

The anima promised.

Also, it gets harder the longer he stays in there. Try to get him through it as quickly as possible. The King may not be generous with his oxygen.

"And then what?" he asked.

"Then you'll enter the labyrinth. And I'll start praying."

Theseus looked down at his arm. It still throbbed with pain, but the skin appeared to be unblemished. "What about the marking? How's that going to help?"

"Wolfram has an exceptionally high sensitivity. The marking – my words – will show itself to you when you need it most."

Theseus paused as they emerged from one of the corridors and the vast, translucent dome came into view.

"And if," he took a deep breath, "I mean, when, I defeat the Minotaur… what happens then?"

"Leave that to me," said Ria.

Theseus did as Ria asked and left the equipment room empty-handed, though when he'd seen his fellow challenger, Theseus Four, equip himself with full body armour and a meduse machine gun he'd been sorely tempted to slip a knife into his pocket.

Don't you dare! his anima had hissed.

Outside, both he and Theseus Four were met by a few disinterested onlookers. They laughed when they saw that he wasn't carrying a weapon. "This is a first!" one of them said, smirking. "What are you equipped with, luck? You'll need it!"

Theseus stood tall and ignored them. Out of the corner of his eye he could see Ria. She nodded and gave him a thin smile of encouragement. Then both Theseus and the other challenger were inside the labyrinth and the trials had begun.

Theseus was being pressed on all sides by people, shouting and calling to each other, their cries desperate. A middle-aged woman tugged at his tunic. Her tear-stained face was somehow familiar. Someone – a child – was howling, either in pain or grief; the keening tunnelled its way into his mind and grated on his nerves. He found himself being pushed this way and that by the crowd; the bull's head became distant and slipped out of view. He tried to force himself through the crowd but it was hard, hot work, and he wasn't making any progress. His stomach twisted with anxiety and he began to sweat. As he felt the crowd weighing down on him, his legs gave way and he found himself face to face with the crying woman. He recognised her – she was his mother!

"They're coming!" she said. "Try to get away!"

"What are you talking about?" asked Theseus, his heart pounding like mad. "Who's coming? The Minotaur?"

"The Magi. Run!"

Theseus felt himself being kicked and shoved; the crowd pressed down on him, made him fall into his mother and crush her. Theseus tried to stand but it was no good, the weight of the people bearing down on him, the terrible anxiety, the worry – was his mother dead? – bore down on him and he became paralysed with panic. If only he had a weapon of some sort. He'd slash at them with a knife and make them move so that he could get some space around him, some air. Oh God, he could hardly breathe. His heart was beating erratically, like it could give up on him any moment, and his lungs were ready to burst. If he had a knife he'd slip it into his throat and kill the panic that way.

Just then there was the sound of gunfire, and for a split-second his mother and all the people around him vanished and there was just the empty dome. And contestant number four sprawled on the ground. Dead.

Then all the people were there again with their insistent noise and weight, their shoving, their panic, once again filling him with the sense that he was utterly trapped. Theseus continued to fight for breath.

"It's not real," Theseus tried saying to himself, remembering that only a moment ago the dome had been empty. "None of this is real. Get a grip and get moving!"

But Theseus couldn't get up. He felt his legs being stamped on, more weight on his back, and he knew that any second now he was going to be crushed to death. And he didn't care.

His anima arose. She spoke to Theseus in a calm, measured voice: *Slow your breathing. Focus on your breathing.*

Theseus did as she said and he found the pain in his lungs lessening. Some of the weight on him lifted.

That's it! Calm your breathing.

As he slowed his breathing the crowd began to thin. He was, at last, able to roll off the body of his mother who was, indeed, dead. Tears seeped from Theseus's eyes and then he remembered Ria's marking.

The small, neat stitches – made in wolfram-rich thread – glowed silver and read: *This too shall pass.*

Really? thought Theseus. *That's it? My mother is dead, and that's all the help she could give me?*

He closed his eyes and exhaled deeply. "I'm sorry," he said, more to himself than his mother. "I'm so sorry."

And when he next opened his eyes, his mother and most of the people had gone. Theseus could once again see the bull-headed beacon. But his mother was dead, and so what did it matter? He sat there for a long time, numb. Eventually, he got up and then walked in the direction of the Minotaur. The remaining people faded away.

Theseus walked on, but without any warning it became dark. He stopped, unable to see a thing. Then two crescent moons came into view above a jagged outline of mountains. Stars appeared. There was the sound of running water in the distance, and behind him, sly laughter.

Memories flashed across his mind, one of them kept recurring and got stuck: his older cousins – brother and sister – taunting him about his height. *Aw, it's our baby cousin, off to the mountain gods to beg for the gift of growth.*

Theseus felt like a young boy again, unable to hold back his childish emotions. Shame flooded through his body and he crouched, his arms around his knees. Not now. He couldn't be dealing with this now.

He remembered turning and standing tall. *My father says I'll be as tall as him one day. When I'm grown up. Then I'll be a General like him and fight the Magi!*

So you admit that you're still a little boy? asked the girl.

Theseus didn't know how to answer. *No,* he began, *I'm just—*

Tell me, continued the girl, flicking her long hair, *are you little all over?*

The siblings approached and he felt his heart drumming like crazy. But he stood his ground.

What do you mean? he said.

They told him to sit with them, to lie down with them; to show them how much of a man he was. And then they were touching him in places that he both did and didn't want to be touched; he found himself simultaneously thrilled and reviled by what their young adult hands and mouths were doing to him. And as his body climaxed and then released, covering his stomach in his own stickiness, the siblings backed away and then laughed at him.

Ew, you're disgusting! the girl sneered, her voice echoing around his head.

He felt sick with shame.

Don't you dare tell! hissed the brother.

Or we'll say that you were the one touching me, said the girl.

They ran off to leave the boy to his shame.

Theseus, crouching in the dome and frozen to the spot, wanted the memory gone. He shivered with sweat. But there it was again. And again. On loop. He looked at Ria's marking: *This too shall pass.* But it wasn't true, was it? This memory was always with him, would always be with him. In here it was amplified; impossible to dismiss. Disgust flung him to the ground, made Theseus slam his head into the floor. Then the back of his head began to itch and he instinctively put his left hand to the itch. He felt for the chip beneath his skin and sunk his fingernails into the flesh. For a moment the memory was gone and he felt relief. But soon enough it was back again, flooding him with shame.

He scraped at the skin, and again he received respite. But not for long.

More scratching; this time his fingers came away wet with blood.

Stop it! cried his anima. *Otherwise you'll bleed to death.*

Theseus's hand hesitated, but then the memory was back and he felt compelled to yank at the flesh once more.

Please stop! begged his anima.

Theseus didn't stop.

What about the Minotaur? You're here to destroy it!

But Theseus was possessed by the memory and compelled to gain relief from it in any way he could.

What about Ria? The marking?

"It's useless," Theseus muttered. "Less than useless."

Again came the memory, the cousins and their taunts; the hungry look on their sly faces. As Theseus was about to pull at the flesh at the back of his neck again, his anima told him to get rid of it then.

Get rid of what?

The marking. Or are you too weak, too childish, to do so?

For a moment he hesitated. Then he moved his left arm away from the chip at the base of his skull. With his weak hand, his right hand, he clumsily tore at the marked flesh of his left forearm, even managing to catch hold of one of the wolfram-rich threads. The pain of the act took his breath away and for a moment drove everything else from his mind.

Now walk.

Theseus instantly obeyed and, somehow, the memory stayed at the periphery of his consciousness.

That's it. You're going in the right direction. Away from the memory.

As he continued to walk his mind cleared and slowly the darkness lifted. It was just him, alone in the labyrinth with his shame, his face wet with tears.

The closer he got to the beacon the better he felt. In fact, he felt amazing, euphoric. He could do this, he could defeat the Minotaur. He started to run. But the closer he got to the beacon the less it looked like it did before. It started to morph into something else and move, walk about. Like a human. Theseus slowed. But it wasn't any human, it was Sophia. His heart raced and his mouth became dry. He knew it couldn't actually be Sophia, the woman he'd loved with such an intense passion all those years ago, still, he longed to spend just a moment with her again, and so he went to her.

We're going the wrong way, hissed his anima. *That's not the way to the Minotaur!*

Theseus ignored her and caught up with Sophia.

The air was warm and he could hear the cry of seabirds. Sand stretched out before him and waves lapped at the beach he found himself walking on.

Sophia paused and smiled at him coyly. She lifted the thick braid of blonde hair that fell down her back over her shoulder. Toying with the wispy ends of it, she asked Theseus how he was.

Theseus took a deep breath. He'd gone through this conversation so many times in his head that he knew exactly what to say. He was fine. Doing well. In command of his own unit. But how about her?

Sophia sighed. "Things are… complicated."

His heart thrummed with excitement.

She told him that things were tricky between her and her husband. He didn't really understand her. She felt so trapped. Like life was all responsibilities and arguments. She wished things could be fun again. "Like they were when we were young…"

Sophia stopped walking and looked up at Theseus, her large, silver eyes mournful yet coquettish. Suddenly she squealed with excitement. "I know!" she said. She began to take off her tunic. "Let's go for a swim!"

And before Theseus had a chance to respond, she'd stripped off her clothes and rushed into the sea.

Theseus quickly pulled off his tunic.

Don't you dare follow her! said his anima. *She's like a siren. She'll lure you to your death.*

But Theseus, overwhelmed by desire, couldn't see any harm in having a little fun.

They waded through the shallows and splashed each other. Theseus tried to keep his greedy eyes off her naked body, but it was impossible. And what did it matter anyway? None of this was real, was it?

Sophia suddenly cried out. "Something bit me! It hurts!"

"Here, let me help," said Theseus, going to her.

She fell into his arms and lifted her leg out of the water.

"See," she said, pointing to a small gash of red.

Theseus could see, but he also knew it was nothing.

Sophia's lovely face was only inches away. It would be so easy to just…

Theseus! cried his anima. *This feels wrong! Don't you – we – have a wife?*

Theseus jerked his head back.

Yes, I remember now, said his anima. *You need to stop this!*

Theseus remembered now too. An image of his grief-stricken wife, her trembling fingers stroking the fine wool of a baby's hat, appeared before his mind's eye. A sob escaped his throat.

Sophia became like lead in his arms and her golden hair billowed upwards as the sand beneath her feet disappeared and she fell away from him, down, down into the fetid depths of the sea which was now more like oil than water. Theseus stumbled backwards, the air knocked out of his lungs. He shivered.

Grief enveloped him, filled his eyes and ears and mouth with its cloying emptiness, its awful weight. With perfect recall he remembered the message his wife had sent him through the cloud: *The Magi destroyed the hospital. Our baby was stillborn. Come home.*

He hadn't wanted to leave his unit; the new recruits were so young, so inexperienced, and besides, how could he comfort his wife when his mouth was thick with grief, his heart a stone?

They'd buried the child, but not their grief. It grew, forming a barrier of thorns between them. And when he'd returned to his unit most of his men were dead, massacred by the Magi. The bodies of his soldiers stared up at him, reproachful. *Why did you leave us when we needed you most?* the lifeless men called out.

Then the spectre of his father appeared by his side. "You'll be a great leader, one day, son. King, maybe. But I fear you've inherited my one weakness"

"What do you mean?" Theseus asked.

"The melancholia. The infinite sadness. It will always be with you. Learn to embrace it. You'll have to if you want to defeat what's ahead."

Theseus willingly lay back in the oily sea and let himself be pulled down.

He's wrong, cried his anima. *It's not a weakness. It simply is what it is. And it does pass. It always passes. Remember the marking!*

But Theseus couldn't hear her. The awful heft of his sorrow had smothered her.

Hours passed. Theseus's full bladder emptied itself. He didn't care. What did it matter? What did any of it matter? His mother was dead. His father was dead. His soldiers were dead. His dear, sweet son was dead. His wife no longer wanted to know him. His breathing became ragged.

His anima, cut off from him, didn't know how to get through to Theseus. She needed to be louder, much louder. Though she spoke to him with all her might, he still couldn't hear her.

She needed another voice. Two voices, three. The voices of the whole dignity culture. The collective unconscious.

That was it!

She called to her brothers and sisters of the individuals that made up Theseus's society. And they came, and they roared.

Wake, Theseus! Wake!

As Theseus began to rouse, his anima told him to arise. *The marking on your forearm is right. This too shall pass.*

Theseus looked down at his arm and saw that it was glowing. It spread warmth around his body, gave him the energy to sit up.

Now, get up, his anima commanded. *And start walking. You don't have to go far. Just start with a few steps.*

Theseus stood and took a few faltering steps. "I can't do it," he muttered.

You can and you will, said his anima.

So Theseus did.

Drop by heavy drop, the oily water fell from his body.

The Minotaur was only a short distance away. A few dozen strides, at most. But Theseus paused. He knew there'd be one last test.

"I don't want to," he said, shaking his head. He didn't want to ever again experience what he'd just now been through.

One last challenge, said his anima. *You're strong enough. We're strong enough. It's just one more thing to get through and then we'll have defeated the Minotaur. And you'll be King. Able to govern justly. You can end the cruelty of the labyrinth.*

Theseus took a deep breath and then stepped forward.

Ghostly faces rushed at him, bringing with them feelings of regret and guilt. Some of the spectres were women with whom he'd had relationships. He'd hurt every one of them, but justified each harmful act of self-interest with the excuse of his past, because of what had been done to him as a child. Shame flooded through him.

Then there were the faces of those whom he'd hurt with words; the venom of his barbed insults making his gut twist with regret.

Last came the civilians, the soldiers. The thousands of humans who'd died in the labyrinth.

The weight of the guilt made Theseus gasp and fall to his knees.

He looked up and saw the Minotaur ahead of him. Its bull head was changing again. It became the head of a Magus and began to speak to him:

"You've called for a truce. Very well. We're not averse to the idea of negotiations. What do you propose?"

Words issued from him. "You've abducted and killed so many humans." Theseus tried to keep the anger out of his voice, yet he felt sick with rage. This was the one chance he had to stop the violence, the never-ending battles. What if he failed? He inhaled deeply, trying to keep his voice level. "Why?"

The Magus laughed. "I don't like open-ended questions. Still. Unlike all the greater species and more advanced beings – the AIs, the Norganics – your mental weakness and seemingly random behaviour makes for fascinating research. We've been studying you, though I admit the macro research – how large swathes of you humans respond to aggression – has only given us a limited amount of data."

Theseus's mind opened to this new knowledge and he frantically searched for solutions.

"So it's information you want? About how we function?" Theseus asked.

"Yes."

Theseus wanted to say something about ethics but then thought better of it. Think, he told himself. What, after all these decades, did they know about the giant Magi? What was their weakness? They had none. They'd tried every kind of weapon against them.

At the edges of his memory something fluttered, just out of reach. He suddenly realized what these memories were: bedtime stories and old wives' tales.

"Well," Theseus said, "let's just say that your research is… unpalatable to us. We want it to stop."

The Magus laughed. "The research won't stop until we get the information we need."

They were at an impasse. Theseus felt the seed of panic growing in his chest and tried to calm himself. The stories were again in his ear. Of the old, old gods. How they overthrew the Gigantes with their tools of war: the shield, the staff, the thunderbolt, the arrows. Then there were the current rumours of a felled Magus, wolfram buried deep in its mountain-sized heart.

"We are amassing our supplies of wolfram," Theseus hazarded, watching the face of the Magus closely.

There it was: the momentary shudder of fear. His bluff had worked.

"So," Theseus continued, "I suggest that your research comes to an end."

The Magus eyed Theseus. "How about we study individual humans instead? In a series of tailored experiments? Mindtours. The battles would stop, and we'd still get the data we need."

"How about you just stop altogether?"

The Magus threw back its gigantic head and then roared at Theseus. "We could wipe out your entire corner of the galaxy – the whole galaxy – if we so wanted!"

Fear sheared through Theseus as the monstrous words reverberated through his body, but he stood his ground.

"How many do you want to study?" he asked quietly.

"A billion."

"No!" Theseus spat. "One hundred." He tried to push the image of sending one hundred humans to their deaths out of his mind.

"A million."

"No." Theseus took a deep breath. "One thousand."

"A million."

"One thousand."

"One hundred thousand."

"One thousand."

The Magus glared at Theseus.

"Ten thousand," said Theseus through gritted teeth.

"One hundred thousand."

"Ten thousand."

The Magus sighed. "This is getting tedious. Very well."

"And you promise to stop at ten thousand?"

The Magi claimed to be of an honour culture – though there was nothing honourable about their experiments – so Theseus pressed him on this. "And then you'll leave us alone for good?" said Theseus. "Do you promise?"

"Yes," said the Magus. "As long as you do not breathe a word of this to anyone."

Theseus thought for a moment. The bargain as it stood was bad enough, but the added secrecy made it even worse. And all because the Magi saw any concession to an enemy as an abominable weakness. "What happens if I die, or get deposed because of your 'experiment'?"

"Then we'll start all over again. With another ten thousand."

Theseus nodded slowly, felt the weight of the secret agreement settling on his shoulders. "Very well."

The head of the Magus disappeared. The memory receded and Theseus was all by himself in the dome, the static beacon of the Minotaur only a short distance away.

Go to it! said Theseus's anima. *Take hold of the bull's head and destroy it.*

Theseus hesitated.

Do it!

Confused, Theseus wondered about what he'd just experienced. Was it truth, or fiction?

Do it!

Theseus rushed to the head which was once again morphing and changing. It began to expand and pulse with immeasurably dense, invisible matter. Theseus knew what it was. It was a singularity. The God point. For an instant he thought he saw a face within the mass, the mouth a giant yawp. Was it God? Or the face of a Magus? Gigantic hands – or were they branes? – flew through the void and as they clapped together the point exploded, expelling matter and heat and force.

Theseus flew backwards, the heat flowing through and around him. The pressure was immense and he gasped for air, thinking that surely this was the end. Yet it was not. The pressure reduced and he shivered as he felt himself cooling. There was movement around him, an invisible swirling, and out of that swirling came gas, which then clumped together to form clouds. Out of the clouds stars were born.

Theseus understood what he was witnessing. It was the birth of a universe, possibly *his* universe. And it was beautiful. Stars grew bigger and more numerous, drawing planets to them. Galaxies were created. He sat up and looked on in awe as the universe expanded, numinous before him.

Then the melancholy was back, just like before, but somehow bigger and more folded in on itself; the dull, oily heaviness expanding from deep within his heart. How small he was. How impossibly small and inconsequential. He was too small to contain this infinitely heavy mass.

Galaxies began to move away from each other and drift apart. Everything was coming undone and unravelling. The God point was now a filthy, grinning rictus, a dirty great black hole sucking nearby planets into its greedy mouth.

Theseus looked at his forearm and saw the words *This too shall pass* glowing. The letters loosened themselves from his skin and floated away, a meaningless jumble. His thoughts, too, drifted apart. His anima attempted to call out to him, but Theseus didn't respond. He was coming apart, just like the universe, his mind unravelling.

Theseus began to laugh, feeling madness upon him. He stood and then ran towards the giant yawp, the monstrous black hole. He would throw himself into it. End it all. But as he came closer, it began to morph and change once more. Into a human. Recognition dawned on him, and his mind started to come together again, his anima deftly weaving all the fragments together and putting them back in place.

The universe around him vanished. He was in the labyrinth, all alone. Facing the Minotaur, who was himself. Theseus shuddered. The final test.

Kill it! cried his anima. *Kill the illusion the Minotaur has created and be done with it!*

But how to kill oneself? Theseus closed his eyes and put his hands to the being's neck. He squeezed and squeezed but there was no give in the metallic throat. He let go, panting, his eyes still closed. He couldn't do it. He wasn't strong enough.

The thread! said his anima.

Before Theseus could stop to think about the pain he pulled the thread from his forearm, the heat excruciating, and then wrapped it around the Minotaur's head and began to pull. The thread went through the metallic neck as though it were molten. At the last moment he opened his eyes to see his own head fall to the ground and turn into that of the Minotaur's.

Theseus fell to his knees, utterly broken.

Arms were lifting him and carrying him. Ria was in his ear. "You've done it! I hoped you would, but I wasn't sure."

"I…" said Theseus, his voice hoarse, remembering who he truly was. His parents weren't dead; he'd seen them only a short while ago. He thought of his childhood – he'd never been abused. And he didn't have a wife, had never had a wife, or a child, and he'd never been in love with a woman called Sophia. "I'm remembering…"

"Shush, there's no need to speak. I'll get you food and water. You've been in there a long time. Inside the King's filthy mind. But he's coming now. This is the moment of triumph. Leave the talking to me."

"They weren't my thoughts," said Theseus. "Nor my memories? None of them?"

Ria snorted. "That wouldn't be much of a test, would it? But touring through someone else's mind – especially someone as fundamentally broken as the King – is another matter. I wouldn't do it."

A bugle announced the King's arrival, and Ria, surrounded by a number of royal guards and emboldened by Theseus's win, proclaimed that King Aristotos's reign was at an end. She lifted Theseus's heavy arm. "There is a new king. King Theseus!"

"Is that so?" said Aristotos, his eyes full of sorrow. "Give me a moment with this challenger."

Ria was loath to step away, but she did – there were enough guards and onlookers about to ensure Theseus's safety.

The King put his mouth to Theseus's ear. "You are challenger number 9942. Only 58 away from 10,000," he whispered. "Ever so close to such a big number."

Theseus once again saw the Magus in front of him and remembered their bargain:

What happens if I die, or get deposed because of your "experiment"?

Then we'll start all over again. With another ten thousand.

"You understand?" asked the King.

Theseus slowly nodded. A single tear ran down his face.

Aristotos took the wolfram thread out of Theseus's hand and then turned to Ria, his face grim. She stared back at him, undaunted.

Aristotos pocketed the thread and went back to the safety of his own guards. "The challenger entered the labyrinth with no weapon, but it appears that he was not unarmed. He had concealed a mighty weapon within his body." The King glared at Ria. "Let it be known that this is against the rules! Those colluding with him will be punished."

"But he destroyed the Minotaur. That's all that matters!" argued Ria.

The King forced a smile, then addressed the crowd. "But as I am a generous man, I will let the matter drop. This challenger has, indeed, done well to destroy the Minotaur and escape the labyrinth. And as I have promised, any challenger who defeats the Minotaur shall be King. If he so wants."

Ria grinned.

The King clicked his fingers. Two footmen appeared; one was holding a cushion on which there was a crown – the King's coronet – and the other was holding a goblet which was full of a red liquid.

"But Theseus may not want to be King," he said. "He may not relish the deathly weight of the crown. The burden of leadership. It may, in fact, be the last thing he desires. You see, the Minotaur has the ability to break people, to go on breaking people for the rest of their lives." The King considered the goblet. "Instead, Theseus may want a swift release from the horrors of the labyrinth by drinking of the poisoned wine. He may choose oblivion, if he so wants. The comfort of death."

Theseus was silent, unmoving.

"Take the crown!" urged Ria. "Take it!"

Theseus went forward, but instead of lifting the crown he picked up the goblet.

"No!" cried Ria. "Don't drink it!"

Theseus put the goblet to his lips.

This is madness! Weakness! cried Ria's animus, calling to Theseus's anima. *Be strong! Let go of the goblet and take up your crown.*

Theseus had no need of speaking with Ria. His anima spoke to her instead. *We are stronger than you can ever imagine. And we are doing the right thing.*

And Theseus drank.

Teika Marija Smits is a UK-based writer and freelance editor. She writes poetry and fiction, and her speculative short stories have been published in *Reckoning, Best of British Science Fiction* (2018 & 2020), *Enchanted Conversation* and *Great British Horror 6*. A fan of all things fae, she is delighted by the fact that Teika means fairy tale in Latvian.

www.teikamarijasmits.com

Fit for a King

Gary Gibson

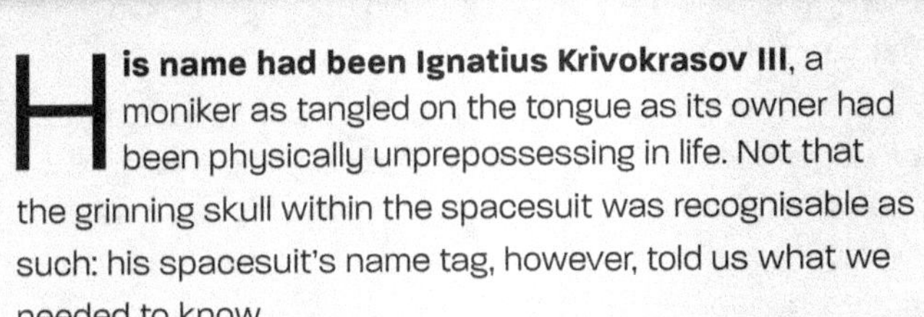

His name had been Ignatius Krivokrasov III, a moniker as tangled on the tongue as its owner had been physically unprepossessing in life. Not that the grinning skull within the spacesuit was recognisable as such: his spacesuit's name tag, however, told us what we needed to know.

"It's him, all right," said Markowski from beside me. "Positive ID on his ship as well."

The asteroid was barely a hundred metres across: no room to land a prospecting vessel of the type in which Krivokrasov must long ago have escaped. Our own ship, a two-man survey vessel, lay hidden behind the ragged curve of the asteroid's horizon.

"There's a ship?"

"About two klicks out, in a matched orbit. Looks like a hunter-killer wiped out its main fusion drive. He'd have known it was all over." He nodded at Krivokrasov's body. "That ... thing he's sitting on. What is it?"

Krivokrasov sat propped up on a chair fashioned from the very rock of the asteroid itself. It was extraordinary, high-backed with intricate details worked into it. The laser-cutter used to fashion it lay nearby, as if it had slipped from Krivokrasov's grasp only moments before. I pictured him working feverishly, one eye on his oxygen supply as it slowly dwindled.

His left arm lay flat on a seat rest, but his right arm and middle finger were raised high, in a gesture aimed, it seemed to me, at the entire universe.

"I think," I said, not quite believing my own words, "it's a throne."

And it was a throne, I realised – one fit for a king, carved from out of a billion-year old asteroid caught in the void between Mars and Jupiter. But why—?

Only then did I remember the famous cartoon used for propaganda by the Earth authorities, showing a bulbous-nosed Krivokrasov squatting on a throne atop an equally ridiculous and minuscule rock, imperiously declaring Ceres to be independent.

Laughing at him. Laughing at us.

I thought of the failed uprising, of the fleets of sentient hunter-killers Earth had sent deep into the Belt. Krivokrasov had disappeared, leaving behind rumours that he was plotting the revolution from Ceres or hiding out in some abandoned base in the Jovian moons.

Instead he had died out here, alone amidst the stars. That cartoon must have weighed heavy on his mind.

"I guess he had the last laugh," I said, a bottomless sadness welling up within me.

Stepping past me, Markowski picked up the laser cutter. To our mutual surprise it flared into life, my visor darkening in response.

"Well," he said, "we can't leave him like this. Drag his body to one side and let's slice that damn throne up."

"What?" Something tightened in my chest. "Why?"

Even through his darkened visor I could see my supervisor – my Earth-born supervisor's – baffled expression. "Can you imagine what the rockheads would make of this? Ignatius Krivokrasov, twenty years dead and still giving Earth the middle finger. Fuck me, it'd be a propaganda coup for the belt."

Ridiculous, I was about to say, then thought again: whether or not Krivokrasov's middle finger in actuality pointed at Earth during the asteroid's long, slow spin around the sun didn't matter. Any rockhead who saw it would know immediately towards which point in space the gesture was intended.

"I lost family during the uprising," I grated, my tongue thick with emotion. "A hunter-killer blew through the seals on an asteroid warren."

"I'm sorry to hear that," he said, not sounding sorry at all. "Here." He passed the cutter to me. "You do it. I'll move the body."

Something shifted deep within me as Markowski moved to drag Krivokrasov from his throne: something I hadn't felt since my foolishly idealistic youth.

"Don't do that," I said, only then realising the threatening manner in which I held the laser cutter.

"Hey. I gave you your orders, rockhead. So do them."

I looked back at Krivokrasov's upraised finger. What you gonna do? His grinning skull seemed to ask. Jump to like a good little slave? Or ask why he's the boss and you're not?

"I think," I said, stepping back, "people should see him just as he is."

I didn't expect Markowski to try and grab the cutter back from me. All I remember is his puzzled expression after the beam sliced through his suit, spilling his blood – and his life – into the vacuum. I didn't even know what I'd done until after I did it.

I stared again at Ignatius Krivokrasov the Third, and imagined that grinning skull performing a slow nod.

Now it's your turn to ask who should be running things around here, he seemed to say, and I found myself nodding in return.

Gary Gibson is the author of a number of science fiction novels sufficiently successful that someone probably hates him for chopping down all the forests used to print them. He hails from Glasgow, Scotland but now resides in Taipei. He has a website at www.garygibson.net.

CAST LONG SHADOWS

Cat Hellisen

The Penitent's Tower

Cat Hellisen

From the outside, the Penitent's Tower is squat and imposing; black stone and a bear pelt of mosses in orange and green. It stands alone on its nub of hillside and looks down on fallow fields. I first saw it at age sixteen as the caravan of coaches and horses and treasure brought me to your rolling lands. I was a replacement bride, an unexpected sister. I was in mourning fierce and wrathful, determined to hate this bittergreen country.

I would love you, I told myself. And nothing else. I would save you from a fate like mine.

I didn't even know you and already I thought I could set you free.

The coaches had travelled hundreds of miles along the roads that webbed and divided the eight duchies of Vestiarik. I had come all the way from Petrell, far to the north east where the world was half underwater, where forest rose out of frozen lakes and where old gods still walked under old wood. The duchy of Jurie was warmer, greener, and the trees fluttered welcome, the lamb-lands sweet and grassy. The cities and villages we passed were bright as painted toys, rain-washed, smelling like rising loaves. My father took us through them all, burdening his wagons with trinkets and books. At night we would eat in the houses of farmlords and borderlords and riverlords, and we were welcomed. Everyone knew who I was going to be when I grew up.

I think you understand that much. We never had a choice. There was no chance for us to find out what we would become. We were bred and moulded and bartered. My sister was going to be your stepmother, and I was held in reserve, ready to be neatly tied to whichever family my father believed would best benefit the Petrells. I was never meant to come to you dressed in engagement gowns, sitting on a wagonload of gifts for your father. I was still weeping, I was still filled with guilt. And the closer we drew to your castle, the more I realised how out of place I was. The deep forests were gone here, the bears and wolves eradicated.

This was never my story.

It was the Penitent's Tower that held me and made me hope I would find my own place. In all that gilded splendour it was the one thing that stood out, raw and rotten. I remember asking my lady-in-waiting what it was, and she told me that it was the tower where traitors were sent before they were executed. So, you see, you are not so civilized after all.

The tower is different on the inside. I am right at the top in the rooms below the conical roof, and though the windows are too small to slip through, I can see the whole of Jurie spread out around me like a map. It is so very beautiful, even now. There, to the north, the violet ridges of the mountains, their caps permanently white, their robes of aspen and apple falling down to their ankles, trimmed in gold and saffron. The seasons are changing fast, the nights crack with frost. It can get very cold up here.

I don't suppose I shall have to worry long about that.

For the most part I try to look to the horizon and the distant forested mountains where I wanted to escape to. Better than to look down, dizzy, and see what is waiting for me. Below is the square, and the scaffolds and wood that the men are bringing hour by hour. The ground is silver wet in the morning and the faggots must be damp and black and soft as autumn earth. Perhaps that is a mercy. Is it yours? Do you want me to breathe in smoke and die unconscious, never feeling the flames? It would be like you to show mercy. But not so likely when you have Lilika whispering in your ear. I wonder what she tells you about me. Some of it is probably true, but there has never been a cat so good at snarling up the truth as your friend Lilika. How does she look to you, I wonder, through that blinded eye of yours? Do you see what she is?

There is someone knocking at my door. It's amusing, these little pretences. Whoever it is, they will curtsy and call me pretty names even while they make my pyre ready. I can't open my own door, but I can draw myself straighter and wear my duchess mantle and tell them, "Enter."

"My lady," the woman says, and she sinks so low I think she means to be mocking. But she looks scared enough. After all the rumours that fly through the Jurie palace, perhaps she truly believes I could change her into a toad or cast an ill-wish on her just by staring. It's all ridiculous. I have never had any real magic of my own. Just little stolen trinkets that belonged to ghosts, and nothing more than the stitchery women have passed down from mother to daughter for hundreds of years.

The serving woman has brought me food and wine. I'm still not certain why they bother, but because this is my last meal inside the Tower, tradition dictates I be well fed. It is a way of erasing guilt. She sets out my lonely feast and pours me a glass of apple-pale wine while a guard watches from the doorway. "Is there anything I can bring you?" she asks. She doesn't actually mean *anything*, naturally. But it is a gesture, and I will take it. After all, this is my last night to explain myself.

"There is a bundle of shirts in my room," I tell her. "The Lady Genivia will know which I mean. And my sewing kit." My lady-in-waiting Genivia was helping me make shirts for the poor before I was arrested. It's not that I am particularly generous or kind, but I am well-trained. My mother sewed shirts for the men of our lands, and on the day of the dancing girl she would hand them out herself. It's a fine tradition. It keeps my hands busy. "I will finish some, before—" I pause. Before what? There is no point. My hands tremble and I put them in the folds of my skirts so that this woman cannot report to you how scared I am. She will not stand in front of Lilika and tell her how the witch shook as the men dragged broken branches from elder trees into the courtyard below.

"And paper," I say, my voice firm and calm. "And ink and a pen." I will be allowed that. I gave no confession. There was nothing to confess. But it's as traditional for the condemned to write out their final words as it is for them to be given a feast, as though tomorrow brings a wedding instead of a funeral. I have had my share of weddings. I'm done with the farce.

The woman nods and curtsies again before leaving me to my meal. Though my stomach is shrunken, and I don't feel hunger much these days, I pick at the spread before me.

She returns with a small basket filled with these last requests of mine and moves to clear away the remnants of my meal.

"Wait." I stop her with an outstretched hand, and she backs away from me, eyes wide, her breath coming in shivery little rasps. I would laugh. "Please," I tell her, "Leave it for now. I may grow hungry in the night."

She stares at me in disbelief. I can see her mind working and wondering what kind of callous bitch I must be to fear nothing, not even my own end. Lilika has told everyone that I have no heart. That I seduced men and used them, that I tried to kill you and left you blinded in one eye, that I murdered my own son. I like that part especially – how she condemns me for his death, and then in the next breath will tell her rapt audience that my son was proof of my witchery. "He was an abomination," she whispered. "The duchess must have gone on all fours for dogs and bears to have birthed such a monster." She who never saw him. My little wolf-child.

And now here's the proof of every lie she tells about me. I will eat heartily and drink like a slattern, and in the morning I will go to my fire reeling and fatted.

"You may leave," I tell the servant, and then, finally, I am alone. None too soon. Just thinking of that day my son died was enough to almost undo me. And I have sworn I will never weep in front of any of Lilika's spies and lackeys.

It takes me a few moments to breathe through the cold wash of sadness. I never really let myself mourn him, and I probably never will. He didn't live long enough to name and, if we pretend hard enough, we can all end up believing he never existed. No one will mark his name in any histories of the Jurie line. He will be erased. My own name will be a footnote. The second wife of Duke Calvai Jurie. Two dates. No Issue.

Lilika can wear widow's whites. I think it will suit her.

Quickly, I take the topmost shirt, the one nearest to completion, and fold the leftover bread, cheese and fruit into it and knot it closed, making the sleeves into a loop I can sling over my shoulder. My hands shake as I fumble with the knots. I don't even know why I'm doing this. A part of me that I have never been able to kill has always made sure I prepared myself for both the best and the worst. It is a very practical side of Marjeta Petrell Jurie, and I suppose I should have listened to that aspect of myself more often. If I had, there's always a chance I wouldn't be here now, hoping for some last-minute reprieve, or for the door to fall open and all the guards to drop into sleep. I could do with magic now.

A harsh call startles me, and I turn to see a magpie sitting on the ledge of the narrow window. His charcoal head is tilted, and he watches me with one clever dark eye. The candle reflects a tiny sun.

"Come for food, have you?" I ask him softly, and he hops along the ledge, wary, but not yet frightened. I suppose I am not a very frightening figure. What could I do to him? "Ah well," I tell the magpie. "It's not as though I have much use for it now." I move like the passing of years, slowly unknotting the sleeves of the shirt to retrieve a crust of bread. I have no chance of escaping. Even if I could squeeze through these slitted windows, what would I do then? Unlike my little beggar-friend, I cannot fly. "Here." I tear scraps for him and toss them to the stones. The magpie flutters down and begins to peck.

Undeterred by my presence, he finishes his meal, then flaps up to the table to begin searching for more scraps. A second magpie appears at my window, and within moments has joined his fellow. A third, emboldened by their squabbling, perhaps, flies in through the window and onto the table. They pull apart my shirt, spilling the pilfered food like the entrails of some fabulous beast. I wonder if they once belonged to you or your grandmother, if they remember being captives. The three magpies ignore me in order to fight among themselves for the food, and when they have consumed everything, they turn to the rest of the shirts, determined to find some new stock.

There is no more food under the shirts. I could have told them that, but I have never spoken the language of birds. The disappointed magpies tear at the pile of shirts, revealing only my little wooden sewing kit, with my silk threads and my needles, and below that, a single parchment and a tiny, stoppered bottle of deep blue ink.

I chase them off and rescue the last of my belongings. The magpies go only as far as the window ledge, and they watch me intently in case I should reveal hitherto unnoticed mounds of grain and fruits.

"You can't eat paper and ink," I tell them. "Greedy little monsters."

The magpies cry once in unison, and fly away, leaving me alone with the scraps of my life. It is suddenly very cold and lonely here. I did not realise I ached so for the company of anyone, anything. I brush my eyes with my palms. Foolish. Tears are useless in the face of death, and I made my choice. I could have left you. Perhaps I should have. I could have run. Perhaps I should have.

I did neither, and I knew the price.

The pen and nib are heart-achingly familiar. They were a gift from you on my wedding day. I smile at the wooden kit. Genivia must have packed it. I can imagine her arguing with the servant, her words hooked and sharp. Why give a woman in the traitor's tower an entire embroidery set when all she means to do is stitch a peasant's shirt? I slip the kit into the deep pocket of my skirt and take the writing equipment to the table.

Once I've cleared myself a little space, moving aside the empty dishes, and refilled my wine for courage, I write your name.

Silviana.

I cannot call you dearest, as I think we have moved beyond meaningless rituals. But perhaps I should. Perhaps I should tell you that you were always meant to be My Dearest Silviana, and that it took many harsh twists to change the thread of our love to hate.

And I wanted to love you. It seems unlikely, given what has come between us, but that day I arrived at your father's castle, I was determined to be something to you. A friend, if not a sister. Never a mother. The thought was too ridiculous.

I was six the day you were born. After a year of mourning, your father made plans for a new wife, and my own father — always quick to take any deal that worked to his favour — offered up my sister as a bride.

It was a deal quickly done. Despite my family's reputation for certain unsavoury practices, there was no doubt that tying his duchy to my father's was in Duke Calvai's best interest. We held back the east. Useful in times of war. Useful if you planned to make yourself a King.

To my sister and I, still girls, and still in that strange land that only girls can occupy, the upcoming wedding was barely real. It

The last of the light is going, and I have only one candle to see me through this final night. This letter that was meant to be something of an apology that apologised for nothing; it will have to do as it is. Your forgiveness will not change what is done. I must work quickly. Though the autumn nights are long, it will be morning long before I am ready.

The sewing kit wood is satiny under my fingers, and the little latch opens soundless. There are skeins of silken thread and a tiny, enamelled box of amber beads each no bigger than a pill louse. And there, beneath the beads is a bear. It is also amber, but it is old and worn, the tiny sharp face blunted, the rough lines dimmed. I stole this when I was barely old enough to talk, and I have never given it up. Behind the bear's head is a hole wide enough to take a thin leather cord. Bears are our omens, the symbol of my mother's family and the guardians of women. Thousands of years ago some girl wore this as an amulet. Perhaps she was a priestess, or a queen. Or perhaps she was nothing.

It doesn't matter who she was, it matters only that she was. I close my fist about the little bear, warming it until I can feel the fine threads waking under my skin. Clever Genni, to bring me this trinket in my darkest, loneliest hour. It belonged to my sister and it is all I have left of her.

The Penitent's Tower is the first chapter of *Cast Long Shadows* by Cat Hellisen to be published in May 2022 by **Luna Press Publishing**. Luna Press Publishing is a SF&F Indie Press based in Edinburgh, Scotland. We meet Francesca T. Barbini, the founder of Luna Press, later in this issue, where she tells us about how she set up the press, and what it means to her and her family of writers.

This is the first in an occasional series where we feature science fiction indie presses based in the UK.

About Cast Long Shadows

Cat says:

"When I started writing *Cast Long Shadows* I was digging into the overused trope of the Evil Stepmother, and what it might really have meant to be the witch in Snow White: a replacement bride, the shadow of the dead and perfect wife, the mother of a step-daughter she'd never planned for. The more I thought about her, the more I imagined her to be a girl out of her depth, alone and afraid in a court full of enemies. And what if she was never a witch? What if other forces were at work to bring her down?

"And so, sliver by sliver, Marjeta Petrell was formed, and her web ofstories spread out from those initial concepts of the witch with her mirror, her open hand offering death. She went from Evil Stepmother to something far greater than a sum of fairy tale images. She became a person.

"I wanted to write a book that explored female friendships, family, their connections which bring both kindness and pain. And it turned out Snow White was the perfect template for that, odd as it might have seemed at first. There is still magic woven through the story, but I like to think the magic runs darker and deeper, and perhaps a little stranger for it."

About the Author

Cat Hellisen writes fantasy inspired by mythology, the role of the outsider in society, and the broken beautiful. She has lived in Cape Town, Johannesburg, Knysna, and Nottingham, and currently lives in a small town in Scotland, where she spends her non-writing time running around with a Ridiculous Dog, and figure skating (without the dog).

Cat Hellisen's novels include *When the Sea is Rising Red, Beastkeeper, House of Sand and Secrets, Empty Monsters, Bones Like Bridges,* and *King of the Hollow Dark.* Her stories centre around the interplay between blood family and found family, class and magic. Her short stories have appeared in *Tor. com, The Magazine of Fantasy & Science Fiction, Apex Magazine, and Something Wicked, Shoreline of Infinity* and in several anthologies ranging from Lovecraftian to Steampunk to African fiction.

The Keep
Raymond W Gallacher

I t was so still, so quiet, so protected by the outer walls and by the overgrown orchards – you knew when someone had found you.

The muffled noises of the scavenger filled you with apprehension. You knew those sounds were not birds' feet tapping on the lead roof tiles, not foxes clawing near the buried trash, and not the low throated growling of escaped wolves from the reserve.

Human predators are heavy in their movements, even when they have trained themselves to make no noise. There is always the scuffling of worn shoes, the interrogation of curious hands, and when they are close enough to the windows or doors, the sound of strained breathing.

A hungry man is often weak, so he is clumsy. He pulls at the padlocks and the chains, pushes desperately at the great doors under the crumbling bastion arch and, when none of that works,

Art: Olen

he paces around the walls of the old house, looking for a place where he can break in, crawl through, or climb over.

After the pulse, when everything switched off in the blink of an eye and the world unravelled, I survived. The keep – and its supplies – were a happy accident of a kind. I hid, ate from its cellar stores and doused the lights at night for fear of what might be outside. I waited. I hoped. I found the original urge to survive in the expectation of rescue – it never came. My walls became my world.

The keep - Strontian House – was over twelve hundred years old. It was built in a time of fire and steel. By the time of powder it was already obsolete. Abandoned by the era of the all-knowing spider's web of electrons that shepherded every part of our lives, it survived the blink that blew away the web. That net of data was an irrelevance to Strontian. Like me, it endured in simplicity.

I was never hungry from the day I opened its doors and locked them behind me. But it cost me in its own way. Because the keep needed its keeper.

When they became too inquisitive, too determined, too close to getting past the locks and the boarded-up windows, I had no option but to go out and kill them. One, if successful, would draw others – that's how scavengers worked. By the time I killed my third man, it hardly affected me at all. It's true what they say about killing: you get used to it.

I dragged his crumpled body from the gates and towards the dolly. Even in moving the dead, I had become efficient. I already had a place for him, deep in the apple orchard. The roots were too thick to allow for graves, but I dared not go any further than the cover of the trees. Fortunately, there was an old drainage ditch which led down and out of the estate. I had deepened it and hidden the soil and bracken close by. I didn't bother to look at him; just rolled him into the hole and shovelled the dirt over.

He was mostly covered over when I froze. My hands tightened on the shovel. I was so used to being on my own that I knew, *just knew*, the sound of someone else.

There was, of course, no reason for him to be alone. My mistake. I didn't check for long enough. Please, I thought, please don't let it be a child. That was too much, even for me.

I had left my crossbow leaning against the bole of a tree. As I reached for it, I saw her. She was pale and thin with wavy red hair, and was wrapped up against the early autumn cold. In that brief moment, she ran and was soon out of sight in the trees.

I tried to get a glimpse of her while I fitted a bolt to the crossbow. My mind raced. What if she was part of a pack? I was realistic about what I could and could not achieve. Five or six of them were too many.

I had to find her. I had to find her before she brought more.

I hunted through the woods and the overgrown thorns then took the path down to the stream and the single track road. At the end of the road, the sea came into a long inlet. There was a line of fisherman's cottages there. They were made of white painted stone, with grey tile roofs and high garden walls that made alleys between the houses. They should have been empty – like Strontian, they had been abandoned for years - but one of them was not. Wisps of grey smoke curled up from the chimney.

High hedges and wild brambles hid the road to the village. If you were careful, you could get all the way down to the shore without being seen. I crept along, the hedge at my side, edging closer and closer to the pebble walkway that led to the houses, then I dropped to a knee.

I took my time. A patient and quiet man could hear scavengers before he saw them. Violent people were noisy; they liked to burn and break.

The cottages puzzled me. Two of them had smoke rising from their chimneys, but there was no destruction, no trash thrown around. There were nets in the sea. Not drifting, not left behind, but placed recently and with purpose. I stretched out for a better look. There were stone fish traps along the shore. It looked like the ghosts from long before my time, from long before the pulse, had come back to reclaim their homes.

I crouched down into cover and beat the ground with silent fury.

Even if they meant no harm, they would attract others. Eventually, they would put me in a position where I had to fight. If I fought often enough, I would lose.

When my breathing slowed and quietened, I crawled around to a gap in the hedge.

The red-haired woman walked along the track to the cobbled street in front of the cottages. She found the walk hard and limped on her left leg. All of us now are a little broken.

I stood up and blocked her path. Still, I admit, not sure what to do.

She recognised me as I advanced towards her.

"Anne. My name is Anne."

Just hearing that made me stop. I couldn't remember the last time someone had told me their name.

"We'll give you some of what we have," she said. "If you just move on. I have a child. Please."

I slung my crossbow over my back. "I'm not a scavenger. He was breaking into my house. Was he one of you?"

She shook her head. "We gave him food. Hoped he would go."

"It doesn't work," I said. We looked at each other, not knowing what to do or say next. I turned to the cottage close by. "You live there?"

"Yes. We used to come in the summers. It seemed like it might be somewhere better. Away from the city."

I shook my head. "No, it isn't. It's just isolated. There are still scavengers. Large packs sometimes. Go back to where you came from." Before I left, I said, "Don't come through the orchard again. There's no way I can tell if you're dangerous or not."

I left her there and went back to Strontian. I hoped and prayed that she would take my advice and go. Anywhere. Just not here.

The keep was not mine – not by birthright. Nor by purchase. Strontian was bought by an American woman. I had never heard of her, but she had made money on some business app. I never looked at what it was. Her name was Orla Kennedy, I supposed she wanted to buy a part of the old country – all that. Those types come and go.

There was a lot of work to be done on the house with quite a few specialist jobs: discreet solar panels, reinforced doors, shuttered windows, and a deep, dry cellar. Another company came in to stock the cellar just as I finished up the electrics. They brought crates of good wine – better than good as far as I could see. I expected that, but next there was case after case of canned and freeze-dried food too. There were even boxes of what I recognised to be British Army ration packs. Unlike most, you could eat them without adding water, although it was a long time since I'd had to force one of the damn things down.

Did Orla Kennedy know something? Did she know that the pulse was on its way? Or was she just one of those survivalist types, but with too much money?

I never got an answer to that because when the world blacked out, she was on a flight from New York somewhere over the Atlantic. I presume her end was swift.

The pulse? It shocked us.

None of us realised how interconnected we were and how fragile it all was. The transportation system came to an instant halt. Communication ended in a heartbeat. Food stayed in the fields and rotted. Water became contaminated. In a way, we still had plenty, but we fell and kept falling until we separated ourselves into defenders of what there was, and thieves of what we needed.

Stockpilers and scavengers.

When the scavengers wore out the cities, they moved out to the country. I lived in an isolated cottage – an easy target. A pack of five of robbed me, took every can of food and bottle of water I had and left me for dead in my own garden. That's when I came to the house. It was only a few miles away, and I had kept a set of keys, meaning to give them to her when we finally met. But what would never be of any use to her became everything for me.

Strontian was a stone-built, defensible block. It sat on the top of a stunted rise of grass and bracken; the surrounding woods cleared away to make a killing field. In later, gentler times, an orchard was planted in the open space, privacy by then being more important than protection. When the owners could no longer manage its upkeep, the house fell into disrepair and the ancient hedges and apple orchards grew wild.

Unless you were born here, you wouldn't know that the keep existed. It can't be seen from the road and there are no obvious pathways to it. The grounds were left untended for so long that it became one of those fairytale castles, hidden behind a maze of snaring branches and unkempt thorns. In appearance, Strontian House was not fairy tale material. It was stark, high walled, and black as all the sins that it was built upon.

I moved in, locked the great doors and kept the windows boarded.

Like all medieval houses, it was cramped, sometimes oppressively so. Its decoration was traditional: tartan carpets, heavy oak and walnut furniture, tweed upholstery, and open fires. I removed some of the boards from the upper windows but kept the shutters closed. Even when I chose to look out at my little domain, I mostly saw the tops of trees and very little beyond. My world became inward-looking. I had no radio, no television. The house had a library, and my life was pleasant, if contained. I dined on thick stews with tinned potatoes. I drank fine wine. At night, I sat by the glow of a heater and read by candlelight.

I had no real plan except to shelter behind the walls and wait for the world to heal. I could not tell if society was on its way to recovery or not. All I knew was that the scavengers grew in number and became more persistent.

Reluctantly, I looked to my own defence.

The arms and armour room was designed to be a study, thickly carpeted and with low, soft light. It was decorated with billhooks, broadswords, crossbows, a Covenanter's breastplate, a flintlock from the Forty Five. I thought they were nothing more than decorations, just replicas, but when I held a few of these things in my hand, they had the weight of old steel, the pistol's action scorched black. Strontian's builders had plied violent trades in exchange for land and money – why not display the tools with pride?

I did not how to use the swords and the guns had no powder. The crossbow was simple. Point it to the ground, put your foot on the stirrup, draw the string back and let it catch on the cog. Fit a bolt. *Aim.*

The first time I pulled the trigger, I was surprised when it worked. I made an impressive hole in the thick oak door.

There was no doubt that it would kill if I could.

I kept the crossbow near my bed after that.

Mostly, I stayed in the house or within the grounds; I patrolled and watched the coast road from hidden places in the orchard. I filled my nights with tinned food and red wine. Sometimes I couldn't eat read or face the walls any more. Some days I couldn't even drink any more. Solitude is addictive, but like all addictions, it is sickening. My seclusion became a substitute for safety.

Four (or was it five days?) after talking to Anne, I took the path down from the orchard, keeping close to the hedges out of habit. Down at the shore, the houses were still occupied. I had hoped that they would leave; that the quiet would unnerve them. Two children played on the beach, their feet crunching on the shingle. Their voices carried above the lap of the waves. I stood and watched them cast flat stones into the water, mesmerised by the scene's ordinariness.

"You never told me your name."

I recognised Anne's voice even though it made me jump. She leaned against the garden wall, watching me with curiosity rather than apprehension. Her hands were dirty and her face had taken some colour. She looked well.

"John… Just John," I said, glancing at the children. "You should get them inside. It's really exposed here."

"The city's worse."

I walked over and stood a little closer. The houses all had cottage gardens. She'd been turning the raised beds, getting air into the soil. "It's the wrong time of the year," she said. "But it's a start."

A man her own age, her husband, I supposed, came from the back of the house and looked alarmed, then angry. He was dark-haired and strong-boned and had been well muscled once. Now, his shoulders were sunk with fatigue. I slung the crossbow across my back and held my hands up; showed I meant no harm. Anne put her arm around his shoulder and encouraged him inside. "He's sick," she said. "He got a cut, and it's inflamed."

I stood like a fool for a moment – a man who had forgotten how to be an ordinary man. Then I walked over, took his weight, and helped get him back into the house. We put him down on a cot in the living room. He was shaking and covered in sweat. His name was Amir, and he tried to thank me, tried to be decent, even though he was still suspicious. He was weak and relieved to be lying down.

"Aren't there any hospitals?" I asked Anne.

"For the few."

Of course.

"I have anti-inflammatories. I'll bring them."

They stayed even though I wanted them gone. I gave them medical supplies sometimes, then turned back home, not waiting for thanks. I did not want to know them. I did not want them to know me.

Amir got better. He tried to talk to me, but I was short with him and kept my distance. They kept out of the orchard as I asked. Now and again, I left cans of fruit on the beach, knowing that the children would find them and take them home.

I guarded Strontian and my orchard. They fished and they planted. More came. Friends and family, they said. That had been their plan. Their hope. If Anne and Amir didn't come back to the city, then it must be worth a try.

Through a partly covered skylight window, I sometimes watched them through binoculars. There were twelve of them by October, including five children. How very human – to keep making offspring even when the world had collapsed.

I still came out from behind the walls and the woods, patrolled the long coastal path, turned inwards towards the inlet and the sea, then home to the keep. I did not go to the cottages for company. I remained, as best I could, unseen.

The agreement held. I left supplies now and again, and in return they kept away from my orchard and my house. The few times I was sick because I drank too much or let food spoil I wanted to reach out to someone, but I fought that need. Instead, I waited out my sweats and nausea until I could get to my feet on my own again.

On a late October evening, still early but readying for darkness, one of the children saw me take the road up by the hedges. He was about ten, and in all innocent excitement, he ran up after me. I instinctively raised the crossbow. As he got close, I said. "Go on back," and then harshly, "Don't follow me."

He chattered and babbled – the confused stream of a highly-strung child. His name was Rudi and his father was Amir. He tried to tell me more. I shook my head; I didn't want to translate his story. I just wanted him to turn around and let me be. Then

Rudi held something out, *something from his mother*. He was breathless as he said it.

It was a paper packet. Wrapped up inside was smoked fish. He turned and ran again, all the way home, even more breathless and excitable than before.

I ate it all before I even got to my own kitchen. It was the closest thing to fresh food I had eaten in nearly a year.

Almost overnight, autumn turned to early winter. The keep had no insulation, and its solar-powered heating struggled against the cold sea breeze. From my first days in the house, I had decided not to burn wood fires, to avoid any smoke showing. As the nights drew in, dark and damp, I sat in the study with a heater full on and the shutters locked tight. The villagers – that was how I had come to think of them coppiced all around the inlet and piled wood as high as the cottage walls for the winter. They did not come near my woods. I suppose the children were told that I was some ogre from an ancient tale, unapproachable and threatening. It was a better story than a drunk in a dead woman's house.

By November, the trees were almost bare and there was rain on the breeze just about every day. The orchard was reduced to a bleak, naked wood - all the easier to see the square, unnatural outline of the keep deep inside. No, I did not like the winter months. They were hungry months. My wariness increased as the temperature dropped.

In the early morning and late evening, I often sat on the roof behind the low parapets and looked out over the hills and the road that pushed through them. I changed my position now and again and watched the village.

The fish traps were still there and there were a few small boats resting on the beach. Two men stretched out a net on the shingle, then walked up and down, checking it for damage. At the back of the houses, clothes hung on lines and flapped in the cold breeze. Children, wrapped up against the wind, played hide and seek in between the woodpiles and water barrels. There were now about twenty villagers and they were more than surviving; they were thriving. Thriving and becoming an inviting target in my jaded view. A pocket of self-sufficiency could not be anything else except an enticement to the have-nots.

There must be, I supposed, settlements all over the country trying to build a life for themselves. Maybe whole new communities rising from the remnants of old ones. A lot of them would be in places like the inlet, close to the sea but with fresh water from the hills. Kind of how we all started in the first place. I wondered how many of these little outposts would have had to surround themselves with wire or wooden palisades – the ones close to the cities, I'd bet.

There was a time when the civilised people of the cities were afraid of the wild places. Now, we in the wild places were afraid of what might come from the cities. Some fools used to think that civilisation's fall would be their paradise – a survivalist's world. It sounds good until you're sick or facing a threat that you can't beat. It isn't freedom – it's just hard. Hard on our bodies and harder on our souls. No, you can store all the tins of peaches and reload all the deer ammo you want – the pulse, and the fall that came after it didn't ennoble any of us.

I was on the roof cleaning moss from the solar panels when I saw a pack on the coast road. Even at a distance, I knew that they weren't more of Amir and Anne's settlers. You learn. You learn the look of the hungry and the wild.

My heart pounded. I lowered myself down through the open skylight into the upper floor. I grabbed the binoculars from the hall shelf and clambered back up onto the roof again, lay belly down, and caught them in the middle of the viewfield. Maybe fifteen or more. Mostly men, a few women. That doesn't seem like a lot, but packs tended to be men of fighting age. Some walked, some rode bicycles, some drew wheeled contraptions – half cart, half trailer- but they were coming.

It was late evening and growing dark. Through the glasses I watched them stop, then turn off the road and haul their carts up into the high woods north of the inlet. They were smart enough to pick somewhere dry and sheltered from the wind. Scavengers aren't stupid. They're not stupid at all. Their ruthlessness should never be equated with being dull witted – they had just learned to harvest in their own way. Never underestimate anyone who survived that first year after the pulse. They were alive for a reason; the base and the fast were often better survivors than the kind and resourceful.

The hillcrest was covered in spruce. Once a commercial plantation, it was tight-packed and still green. I couldn't see their movements, couldn't guess at their intentions, but I knew the treeline was a good vantage point. They could see the village – and the whole inlet – from there.

I made sure my doors were locked and doused every light. I covered the skylights and closed every interior door. There was nothing I could do except wait. I took the stairs down to the cellar and found a fine wine. A Calon Segur - something I could never have dreamed of owning or opening back before the pulse. Odd how this horror made me a man of taste.

I opened it, let it breathe, and sat by my own cold, dead fireside while I drank it.

Outside, from the hilltop, I could hear the distant noise of the scavenger pack as they made camp. Brutal people make an ugly row. I dozed fitfully in my chair, unable to settle. In those half-awake moments, I prayed to a God I no longer believed in, "*Let them pass me by.*"

All I wanted were my walls and my wine cellar, my cloying tinned stew, and to be left alone. Guilt didn't mobilise me; the thought of the children didn't even enter my head.

Don't try to like me and don't try to find some redeeming quality. You will be disappointed.

Let me tell you about courage. Courage is like a bank account. You take from it, and you take from it, and then one day, there's nothing left.

The other side of that is cowardice. You hide behind it, and you cling to it, and you justify it, and on and on it goes. It is much more powerful than bravery, but it, too, eventually runs out. No matter which one you choose, you will exhaust it.

I gulped a mouthful of wine and then a few more. Only then did I pick up the crossbow and head for the door. It was no epiphany. The ogre did not become more human. There was no rediscovery of the hidden man.

I did not find courage. I was not redeemed. I simply could not sink any lower.

With my crossbow on my shoulder and bolts in my belt, I unlocked the keep's side door and gate, then followed the path through the orchard and down to the inlet. The scavengers had found them. Fire lit the village and the sea like gold.

What do I remember? Flashes. Images. Parts too disjointed to be in any real sequence.

The scavengers had set a roof alight as their opening move. Anne and another woman were being held back from the burning cottage. Was anyone still in it? I couldn't know. A man, possibly Amir, was lying on the cobbles, unmoving. One of the fishermen was being beaten. Someone was trying to cover him, protect his head. There were other things that I could half hear but not see. People shouting, screaming in protest as their homes were ransacked. Children crying. Outrage. Fear.

The villagers weren't cowards. They just didn't have that ruthlessness that the scavengers had.

I knelt at the edge of the firelight and took a bead at the big man giving out the beating. He was bulky and barrel -chested, with long braided hair and calf-high boots. I put a bolt straight through his back. Then another through the woman next to him, egging him on. The advantage of surprise was gone after that. I was loading a third bolt when they turned on me.

I fired again. It scattered a few of them, but that was all.

Someone hit me from the side. I grabbed hold, and we both hit the ground together. I was punched – hard. My mouth filled up with blood. Even on the ground I fought on, I punched and clawed. I would have bitten too, but I had lost some teeth and my mouth was numb. A guttural voice screamed, but the words didn't register. Body weight held me down. I smelled unwashed clothes before my attacker was pulled off me. Something that felt like ice followed by flames went deep into my bicep.

I bought time. Nothing more.

I stayed in the village while I healed. Two of the fishers, June and Adrian, had a spare bed in their cottage and put me up there. I was not fit to protest. The room was small but warm. More importantly, it was private; I was in a poor state. The knife blade had missed my artery by a hairsbreadth. Adrian told me that arteries are tougher to cut than most of us believe. He was full of that kind of information. He'd been a theatre nurse once and the closest thing to a doctor we'll see out here. June had been a teacher in the city. She was teaching again, only this time she had paper, old pencils, and the kids around a kitchen table. I am sentimentalising it, perhaps, but, what else do you need?

A few of the villagers were badly hurt, but they were a tough and resilient crowd in their own way. Those who were able went back to work the next day. The burnt-out roof was mended. The nets were repaired and taken out to be cast into the sea.

As for the scavenger pack, they withdrew when their hold was broken. They made a lot of noise and threats, but they were done. They left two dead behind. The villagers buried them – even gave them something of a ceremony. I wouldn't have.

Amir and Anne visited me, fed me on fish cakes and a kind of skillet bread. Others visited too, all faces I did not know then, came to pass time with me. They all had similar stories; all of them had grown tired of waiting and turned their minds and hands to other skills and enjoyed it more than they expected.

Soon, I was well enough to stand and walk without weakness and nausea.

When it was time, I washed and dressed in my laundered clothes and walked out into one of those bright, cold winter days. The children saw me and stared – all curious about the fearful figure from the old house.

I found Amir on the shore. He smiled and seemed pleased to see me on my feet. "You strong enough to be on your feet?"

"Yes. And to go home," I said. "Come with me. Bring a few others too."

"You need help?" he asked.

"No," I shook my head. "Get some baskets and boxes and come up to the house. I have supplies you need."

"We're doing fine," he said.

"You have children. Don't be proud. I have more than enough."

They came, and I opened the doors of the cellar to them. I rested while they filled their boxes. The wine was especially appreciated – I would have been disappointed if it had not been. They all took a share, and I still had plenty.

When the villagers left, I was alone again and glad of the quiet. I was sore and easily tired, but I lit a fire – a real crackling, smoking fire and opened the shutters over the window that gave a view onto the inlet and the sea.

I could have gone to the village. They would have welcomed me.

But no, I made Strontian my home.

The keep must have its keeper.

Raymond W Gallacher is based in Glasgow and writes science fiction by night and business tech during the day. Raymond returned to education after a life changing event and studied The Novel and Short Story at Glasgow University. He has finished his first novel and has a novella planned.

Approaching
Human
Eric Brown

The Disappearance of Jake Carrelli

I spend most of my time in VR, that playground suburb of the Cloud.

I've constructed myself a personal retreat, a place where I go to get away from all the noise. I call this haven the End of the World.

It's a projection of how things might be five billion years from now. The sun is a pulsing cinder sending out its dying heat to an Earth from which most of humanity has fled to the stars. Life gathers around the temperate equatorial region. The landscape has mellowed with age: sweeping green pastures and ancient oak forests and mossy manses where the last old families of humanity dwell. There is no industry, no mechanisation, no *production*. It is the perfect antidote to our times.

I have a small lodge overlooking a saddle-shaped greensward on which timorous deer-like animals graze, and birds call from the woodlands. The planet has slowed in its turning; a day lasts for thirty-five hours now, and the afternoons are long and balmy.

I sit on the veranda, sip sundowners, and admire the view.

I was taking it easy at the End of the World when the black cat I call Sable leapt up onto the veranda rail, arched his back and miaowed. This meant I had a potential client in VR.

I could have quit my retreat and met him or her on neutral VR territory, but I was loath to leave the End of the World. I allowed entry to my realm, and a second later, a figure materialised on the grass before the veranda.

"Nice place you've got yourself here."

"Ed," I said. "Good to see you."

"And you, too, Zorn. How's things?"

"I can't complain."

"May I join you?"

"Be my guest."

He stepped onto the veranda and settled himself in a wicker easy chair.

Ed chose to be himself when he visited me in VR, which I always took as a compliment. He was a big, silver-haired New Yorker, invalided from the NYPD five years back when a crazed gunman made mincemeat of his legs. He'd recovered, moved on, embraced his disability, and became a bigger, better person. Hell, even his avatar walked with a limp.

I'd done some undercover work for him when he was in the Force, and we'd kept in contact since his retirement. He knew I was an AI, but he wasn't prejudiced. I liked him for that.

"Drink?"

"One of those would be nice."

I poured him a long, cold sundowner, and he drank.

"How can I help, Ed?"

He stared across to the setting sun, a great fulminating hemisphere straddling half of the far horizon. Slow ejecta of molten fire erupted from its ruddy hemisphere. I always found the sight soothing, soporific.

"Did you know I had a brother?" he asked.

"I didn't."

"Jake. Ten years my junior. A neuroscientist with an outfit called OmniScience. We were close."

"*Were?*"

"He disappeared, close on a week ago. His wife thinks some rival tech outfit has grabbed him for what he has up here."

He tapped his head. "I pulled a few favours, contacted old colleagues." He grimaced. "Nothing doing. Not a trace. He vanished into thin air."

"No one vanishes," I said, "without leaving a trace."

"Jake did. He was last seen leaving his place of work just before four on Tuesday afternoon and entering a bar. After that, nothing."

"I'll do what I can," I promised.

"I'll make sure it's worth your while, pal."

I shook my head. "I don't want paying," I told him. "This one's on me."

"I insist."

"Payment," I said, "wouldn't make me do a better job. But doing it for a friend, gratis, will."

"I owe you one, Zorn," he said.

"You owe me nothing, Ed. Now, the details…"

I knew pretty soon that it was going to be a real-world case.

I'd dredged what I could from the Cloud, but such was the nature of Jake Carrelli's job – top-secret, hush-hush – that I kept coming up against encrypted security bulwarks and data caches protected behind impregnable firewalls.

So I did some investigating in the real world.

An hour after Ed contacted me, I assumed my avatar outside a plush upstate villa, walked down the garden path, and rang the bell.

Ella Carrelli opened the door, smiling. "Ed told me to expect you," she said. "Please, come in."

I settled in an open-plan lounge with a view over an acreage of lawn which told me that Jake Carrelli had earned big money.

"I'll do everything I can to help," I said, "but I need some information. I've dredged the Cloud, but found little."

"I'll tell you what I can…"

She was small, dark-haired, nervous. She wound the rings on her fingers and shot me quick, darting glances. I knew, intuitively, that she was hiding something.

"Did your husband seem worried at all before he disappeared? Concerned about anything?"

She shrugged, pulled at her wedding ring. "Not that I noticed. He could leave work at work, enjoy what we had here. His work was cutting-edge, high pressure … but it had been like that for years. He could live with it."

"Do you know what he was working on?"

I'd asked Ed the same thing, but he'd just shaken his head.

Ella nodded. "He told me a little about it, yes."

"And?"

She licked her lips. "He was working on consciousness paradigms."

I trawled the Cloud and had it in a nanosecond. "Cerebral templates? Cortex analogues?"

She nodded. "That kind of thing. It was his specialism."

"He was a Mechanist?"

She twisted her lips into a bitter smile. "He didn't like that word. He said it was reductive."

"I'm sorry," I said. "What word would he have preferred?"

"He would have said that his philosophy couldn't be reduced to one neat, pat word or phrase. Put simply, he believed that the human mind could be likened to an AI consciousness. He saw no difference between a biological human brain and a manufactured, sentient, self-aware cognitive nexus."

I smiled, wondering if she knew she was talking to just one of those.

I said, "It's a position that's gaining ground. Did he ever talk to you about how he applied his philosophy to his everyday work?"

She smiled. "He did, once or twice. But he soon lost me."

We talked a little more about his career; how long he'd worked at OmniScience, how he got on with his colleagues. I asked the usual questions. Did he have enemies, envious colleagues, co-workers in the same field who might want him out of the way? She gave the same answer every time: "Not that I am aware."

"Ed said you thought a rival tech firm had— " I began.

She interrupted. "That was just after … just after Jake went missing. I said whatever came into my head. I wasn't thinking straight." She stared at me with tear-filled eyes. "I don't know what happened to my husband, Mr Zorn."

As I rose to leave five minutes later, Ella Carrelli stopped me. "There is one thing…"

"Go on."

"A month ago … he came home one evening, very excited. He said something about a breakthrough, a 'parallel lattice' or something like that. I must admit that it meant nothing to me."

I trawled, but came up with nothing that made any sense.

"He said that he was interviewing someone who might collaborate with him on a project."

"Someone?" I said. "Did he mention a name?"

She nodded. "Jilpa Chiang."

I thanked her, promised that I'd do all I could to find out what had happened to her husband, and quit the villa.

Her personal com pinged as I left, and she took the call. I hacked the communication and listened in as I walked away from the villa.

The upshot was that Ella Carrelli had a lover, and was meeting him in an hour.

As I turned the corner and collapsed my avatar, I admitted that her crocodile tears had taken me in.

I had a couple of hours to kill before I was due to meet Jake Carrelli's boss at OmniScience, so I decided to concentrate on Jilpa Chiang.

A quick trawl gave me more than I could assimilate in a few seconds. It took a full two minutes before I'd taken on board her biography, and another three to parse the resume of her scientific achievements. I pride myself of keeping abreast, but Chiang's work was way out there.

I accessed her VR code, put in a polite request to speak to her about the disappearance of Jake Carrelli, expecting to be fobbed off with a terse rebuttal. World-famous scientists of Chiang's stature didn't waste time with AI investigators, self-aware or not.

So I was surprised, a minute later, when I received an affirmative, accompanied by a private access code and a message: "I can see you here for ten minutes at noon."

I made sure I was there on the stroke of midday.

I know that VR is just a virtual projection of the human psyche, and therefore, nothing in there should shock me – but it did. What Glendon Connelly got up to in the sex club, for instance. And what I found in Jilpa Chiang's private VR domain.

I materialised on a perfect lawn surrounded, in the distance, by pagodas and fir trees. The lawn was peopled by old men in loincloths, all of them iterations of the same bent, grey-haired, haunted-eyed individual.

And then I saw the little girl.

She was seated on a straight-backed chair in the centre of the lawn. She wore a white dress, and her feet were bare. I judged her to be perhaps eight years old. As I approached her, I saw that her face was flawlessly perfect, her huge jet-black eyes set flush with her high cheeks. Her little toes hung inches above the grass.

A whip lay across her lap, gripped in her fists.

All around the lawn, the old men stood in poses of abject apprehension.

"Jilpa Chiang?" I asked.

"Mr Zorn."

Her expression lacked all emotion. She stared at me from the perfection of the avatar of the little girl she had been.

"About Jake Carrelli..."

"I read about his disappearance."

"I understand he contacted you, perhaps a month ago?"

"We were discussing the possibility of working together."

"On...?"

She stared at me. "You're an artificial self-aware entity built on a Zakinthos substratum, running on linear prime directives within Bueler–Sarkosian parameters."

I blinked, flattered by the depth of her knowledge.

"I too do my research," she said. "What I mean is, will you understand me when I get ... technical?"

"Try me."

"Carrelli and I were discussing the possibility of synthesising our specialisms, and working together on a paper correlating recent research on syncretic mind-body theories, concentrating on Carrelli's duality theories and my own post-Bueler hypothesis."

Then she got technical.

I listened, taking it all in.

Five minutes later, she finished and sat in prim silence, smiling at me.

"So..." I said, "let me get this straight. The bottom line is that Carrelli thought that the human mind could be copied, just as the content of an AI mind can be – and is – copied?"

"Crude, but more or less correct." The little girl twinkled her jet-black eyes at me patronisingly. "This was the logical assumption, entirely in line with the beliefs of a Mechanist like Carrelli."

"And you agree with him?"

She tipped her head from side to side. "Let's say that I was willing to give his theories serious consideration."

"So I suppose what I'd like to know, Ms Chiang, is whether his theories might have anything to do with his disappearance?"

Surprising me, she slipped from her seat and stood before me.

"That," she said, "I would not know. I am a theoretician. I exist in a realm of pure thought and rarely consider what you might term the 'real' world. I would advise you to question his colleagues about his disappearance."

"I'll do that," I said.

"By my calculation, your ten minutes have elapsed," she said. "Goodbye."

I thanked her. As I was about to exit her domain, she stepped forward and cracked her whip viciously.

An old man screamed.

"You will obey my *every* word!" the little girl called out.

Angel DiMatteo, the CEO of OmniScience, was a small silver-haired woman in her sixties.

In the steel and obsidian lobby of her corporation, she had her security system check my credentials. Then, satisfied, she gave me a tour of the labs.

She called them labs, but there wasn't a test tube in sight.

It was a hermetic environment with studious techs poring over softscreens and interfacing with smartware cores via headsets. DiMatteo explained the set-up as we went along, but told me nothing I didn't already know.

On a gallery overlooking a lab where cyberneticists were conducting state-of-the-art research into AI consciousness, we paused, and I fired the usual questions. Was Jake Carrelli liked and respected at OmniScience? Did he have enemies? Was he happy in his work?

Carrelli was loved at the company, she replied; he didn't have an enemy in the world, and he lived for his work.

"He was a brilliant theoretician whom we valued highly," she said.

"I understand he was working on syncretic mind-body theories, concentrating on his own duality hypothesis?"

"Based on his Mechanist theories."

"In short, he believed that the human mind could be copied?"

Again, she nodded. "That's correct, Mr Zorn."

"In your opinion," I asked, "do you think it's possible that his disappearance might be in any way linked to his work here at OmniScience?"

She hesitated, and I interpreted her hesitation as suggestive. "If you would accompany me to my office, Mr Zorn."

Intrigued, I followed her.

Installed behind the silver arrowhead of her desk, she steepled her fingers before her stern face. "The day Jake went missing," she said, "OmniScience suffered an unprecedented security breach. We were hacked. I pride myself on having all the latest security software *in situ*, making my company impregnable. Or so I thought. We were hit by a firestorm of such intensity and complexity that our security cordon couldn't cope and went down for just three seconds – but that was all it took."

"All it took?"

She pulled a face, pained at having to make the confession. "To blitz a data cache."

"And by blitz, you mean…?"

"I mean wipe, eradicate, ensure total and irrevocable erasure."

"It must have been a pretty damned important cache for someone to have gone to such lengths."

She regarded her steepled fingers for a long time, considering something, and then said, "Mr Zorn, shortly before he disappeared, Jake Carrelli made a breakthrough."

"In…?" I prompted.

"We succeeded in copying the content of his mind, uploading his entire cognitive assembly to a smartcore within our largest mainframe."

She stopped there, staring at me.

Had I been human, I might have been sweating by now.

"And the data cache that was blitzed?" I asked.

"The hackers ignored everything else – data of considerable value, I might add – and concentrated on just one cache. The cybernetic copy of Jake Carrelli's cerebral identity."

I stared across the desk at the woman. "They wiped it," I said. "But you had backups, I take it?"

She looked uncomfortable. "We made backups, copies, and lodged them in various locations in half a dozen smartcores in the Cloud."

"Don't tell me…"

She nodded. "Whoever did this, blitzed every single one of them, Mr Zorn." She hesitated. "And the three copies that we lodged in cores that were not connected to the Cloud, that were totally independent, were erased too. We're looking at the possibility that that was an inside job."

I digested all this, then said, "Of course, the reason for this blitz was that"

She interrupted. "That's right. They wouldn't have gone to all the trouble of blitzing out smartcore without first copying, for their own purposes, Jake Carrelli's cerebral identity."

That evening Ed Carrelli and I sat on my veranda at the End of the World, and stared at the bloated sun on the far horizon.

"So let's get this straight," he said. "Some hacker, for some reason, blitzed the OmniScience smartcore, but not before they copied my brother's cerebral identity – and a few hours later Jake went missing?"

"'For some reason', yes," I said.

He sipped his sundowner. "So … what's next?"

"DiMatteo gave me all the data she had on the firestorm raid," I said. "I'm in the process of sifting through the information. I have no doubt that the copying of Jake's cerebral identity, and his disappearance, are in some way connected." I hesitated. "I just have to work out how, exactly."

We sat in silence and drank.

Before us, the sun flung solar flares through its magnetosphere in gorgeous, slow-motion arabesques.

Professor Desdemona Lila Taylor says:

"*Approaching Human* is continued online on the Shoreline website in fortnightly episodes with Episode 3: *Played Like a Patsy...*"

All 10 episides of Approaching Human will be published as a novella in June 2022

Eric Brown has published over seventy books. His latest is *Murder Most Vile*, and later this year is the SF novel *Wormhole*, written with Keith Brooke. Also with Brooke, the *Enigma Season* quartet of novellas is forthcoming from PS Publishing. He lives near Dunbar in Scotland.
His website is at: ericbrown.co.uk

The Solarpunk Storytelling Showcase: The Power of Storytelling in Building a Better Future

Lottie Emily Dodd

In July 2021, **Extinction Rebellion's** first global short story competition for all ages was launched. The Solarpunk Storytelling Showcase called on people all around the world to imagine a sustainable and equitable future for our planet and turn it into an engaging piece of fiction.

Solarpunk, the titular theme of this showcase, is a genre of speculative literature and art that envisions a planetary future in which humanity, non-human nature, and technology co-exist in harmony. Our aim was to use the power of collective imagination as a tool against the climate and ecological emergency - because through radical re-imaginings of the world, we can get closer to creating a future that is positive and healthy for all life.

2021's showcase was this project's first iteration. The idea was seeded by myself and Alex Dickinson, and given wings by XR Wordsmiths, a group of XR Rebels battling against the climate and ecological emergency primarily via the written word.

Entrants were asked to consider the following questions and write a short story of up to 2500 words: When you think about the future you want for the planet, what visions does your imagination conjure up? How would human societies interact with nature? How do you think a plant or an animal would describe its place in the world, and how it came to be so? What changes (from the smallest detail to large structural changes or technological innovations) would transform today's world into the world you imagine?

This was our first attempt at creating a writing competition, let alone a global one, so we didn't really know what to expect… but stories soon started flooding in. Tantilising tales of floating cities, Arctic-cooling technology, Solarpunk schools, sustainable communities, utopian hospitals, climate disaster memorial statues… all spectacular imaginings of a post-Anthropocene future in which humanity, non-human nature, and technology are all thriving harmoniously.

The winning entries (3 adults, 3 teenagers, and 3 children plus some additional categories: 'XR Wordsmiths Top Picks, Runners Up, and Honorable Mentions) were announced in December 2021 after being selected by a diverse panel of judges including eco-authors, scientists, teachers, and a UK Green Party politician. These stories are due to be published across Solarpunk Magazine, Solarpunk Society Magazine, Shoreline of Infinity Science-Fiction Magazine, the Rapid Transition Alliance, and in Extinction Rebellion publications.

Other prizes included full scholarships to Terra.do (the world's first online climate school) totalling over £5500, in-person children's eco-design workshops, magazine interviews, Youtube interviews with eco-fiction expert Dr. Lovis Geier, WWF animal adoption kits, 1-to-1 mentoring sessions with eco-poet Helen Moore, Solarpunk Magazine subscriptions, Solarpunk anthologies, wildflower seeds, and audio versions of each story.

All winning stories have been or will be illustrated by a team of artists from around the world: Chile, South Korea, India, the UK, Brazil, the US, and Canada.

The creative domino effect of the showcase did not end there; some of the winning stories have also been adapted into virtual drama workshops by Hamburg-based sociodrama group, Dandelion Spaces, which have so far been attended by over 150 participants tuning in from multiple countries. We certainly hope to launch future showcases and may even plan a future non-violent direct action based on one of the winning stories.

The stories, illustrations, and information about the showcase are now available at solarpunkstorytelling.com, a website hosted on a solar-powered server (thanks to the brilliant work of Tega Brain and Theresa Merchant of Solar Protocol). If you have any questions about the Showcase, please contact xrwriters@protonmail.com. The XR Wordsmiths are also active on Facebook, Instagram, and Twitter.

It was a truly awe-inspiring experience to have this project receive such enthusiastic responses from many unexpected people and places around the world. That so many talented individuals were willing to put in time, effort, and imagination towards a common goal of storytelling-inspired future building has been encouraging to say the least. We hope for the ripple effects of this project to continue for years to come, and for it to spark similar projects in different languages around the world. As such, please get in touch if you would like to create a Solarpunk Storytelling Showcase in your language - we would love to help you!.

Lottie Emily Dodd is Project Lead of the XR Wordsmiths Solarpunk Storytelling Showcase. Her academic background is in East Asian Studies (specifically Japan, China, and Taiwan) and Social Anthropology. She currently works for Terra.do, the world's first online global climate school, and teaches Japanese language to secondary school children.

Art: Dustin Jacobus

The Tides Rolled In

Christopher R. Muscato

The tides rolled in. The tides rolled out. It was as simple as that. And in that simplicity, there was power. Enough to even light entire cities – not that Afton knew personally. Her little village did just fine, roaming the waves, but in her thirteen years she'd never seen the capital of the Floating Republic. She'd never walked on sidewalks so steady it was said you couldn't even feel the rocking of the waves. For Afton, sea legs were the only legs she'd ever known. But today, that would change.

Afton looked down at the scroll in her hands, her eyes hovering over the pliable screen. Her lips twitched, a subconscious reflex as she rehearsed her plan, her thoughts finding shape in inaudible whispers. Then aA breeze blew a stray hair in her face and she suddenly became aware of herself, feeling the subtle burn of embarrassment in her cheeks. Her eyes darted back and forth, assessing whether anyone had seen her talking to herself, seen what was on her tablet. She darkened the screen and rolled up the scroll, tucking it into her belt and leaning against the rail of her ship, mind still turning as she lost herself for a moment in the horizon.

"Ahoy there, matey!" A voice boomed from behind her. "Be ye ready to see the great city?"

Afton rolled her eyes as she turned towards the sound of footsteps.

"You're not going to talk like that in the city, are you?"

"What be ye talking about? This be how all captains speak!"

"*Ayah*. Seriously."

The captain roared with laughter, rubbing his round belly.

"Captain, come look at this," came a voice.

"Duty calls." The captain winked, his voice trailing after him as he scuttled off. "What have ye scallywags done now?"

Afton rolled her eyes again, turning back to the ocean churning rhythmically below the bow of her community. Her young fingers traced the edges of the scroll secured in her belt for a moment, then slowly withdrew it. Her attention snapped in the direction of the captain's thunderous voice, still audible even from the adjacent deck. Afton shook her head and shoved the scroll back into her belt. Despite her father's outwards demeanor, he always said it was a great privilege to be elected captain of a village.

It was also a great privilege to be a captain's daughter, and so Afton diligently bustled about her chores, inspecting rigging and cleaning solar panels as her village plowed through the waves. She checked in on the gardens, murmuring to the plants as she brushed the leaves with her fingers. She stopped by the *ikat* huts and brought tea to the weavers. She followed her father on a routine inspection of village. Even with the new carbon filaments, there was always thatching that could be done on the woven roofs of the many *rumah adat* of the village, from the conical Mbaru Niang of the Wae Rebo deck to the Batak Toba deck's pointed gables. The entire village swayed on its half-submerged piles, and Afton skipped deftly from deck to deck, along rope ladders and walkways, assisting with whatever tasks she could find, stopping only occasionally to smell yams and shrimp boiling in pots of aromatic spices.

There were more than enough things to do in the village, more than enough distractions to keep her mind occupied. And yet, as she scurried from deck to deck, from chore to chore, she noticed that the inner decks and structures were quickly emptying of people. Excitement sizzled throughout the village, a palpable energy that swept people away from their work like a riptide and ferried them to the village's outer railings. It wouldn't be long now.

Afton tried to remain focused, to remain diligent. She tried to ignore the buzzing in the back of her mind, the itching in her fingers that seemed magnetically drawn to the scroll in her belt and the notes and outlines and maps flashing across its surface. She tried. It wasn't long, however, until she could stand it no more and found herself wedged alongside the other children, eagerly scanning the horizon.

Cerulean waves danced before her village, a mesmerizing rhythmic geometry tracing the fine border between sea and sky before blending into a medley of soft blues and misty haze. Beams of sunlight punctured the waves, columns of luminescence streaking defiantly into the depths below. Afton had lived her entire life on these waters. The ocean was their home, their power generator, their garden, and still it never ceased to steal her breath from her lungs. Whenever her father caught her gazing upon the sea, he would say that all the formulas and equations in the world wouldn't mean a thing if they couldn't simply appreciate the beauty of it. Harmony required more than mathematics.

Living among the waves, carried by currents and the natural rhythms of the ocean alongside the fish and the dolphins, over forests of seaweed and metropolises of coral, their village was one with the watery world surrounding it. They had found their harmony, but very soon, the entire village would get to experience this on an entirely new scale.

The city was getting closer. It was hard to imagine that such a place was still able to exist in perfect unison with its ecosystem. The city was just so big.

Incredible as it was to believe, Afton heard that there were once cities even larger on the land, even if most people today lived on the water. Her ancestors had lived in such a city, a long-lost place her grandparents called Jakarta, a name they only spoke of in the reverent whispers of a people eternally in mourning. It was one of many places reclaimed in the Great Flooding.

Her grandparents called it that, although Afton never really understood the term. It didn't sound so great. Entire countries disappeared into the ravenous sea, hundreds of thousands dead and millions displaced by the rising ocean, the survivors moving onto the water as the remaining land dried up and was depleted. Afton had read all about it. She was good at science. All the marine ecologists and engineers and meteorologists in her village said so.

What didn't make sense to Afton was how nobody noticed. Her grandmother said that people were aware the ice was melting but weren't willing to do anything about it, neither to save the planet nor the people, but that made even less sense.

When Afton looked down at her hands, she was surprised to see her scroll between her fingers. She slunk away into a corner to open it, eyes hungrily zipping from side to side. Her lips twitched as she read over the plan, little beads of sweat forming on her brow. She looked around again, ensuring that her father was not watching, could not witness her nervous recitations. Huddled against the wall, the scroll an inch from her nose, Afton read over it again and again.

"There it is!" Someone shouted. Eyes open wide, Afton's heartbeat jumped, and she rose on the tips of her toes to try and see between the crowds pointing and gasping, her small frame weaving between legs until she reached the railing. And there, crystalizing in the distance, magnificent structures began to take shape. The excitement was enough that even Afton's great agenda and responsibilities vanished in her mind, the scroll returning hastily to her belt as eager eyes bulged with wonder.

The village slowed as it navigated the maze of wind and tidal turbines heralding the appearance of the great city itself. Children on the floating village pointed upwards in awe at these awesome structures, children inhabiting apartments on top of the turbines laughing and waving giddily at the passing community. Their cheers joined with the clarion songs of seabirds plunging and diving, skimming the water's surface, frolicking between roosts built into the slowly revolving edifices.

"You know every one of these turbines provides the backbone for an entire ecosystem," Afton informed a young boy who clung to the railings next to her, mouth agape. Afton tipped her head to glimpse a rainbow of brightly colored fish darting between the turbines. "There's all sorts of reefs living down there."

With the village magnetically tethered, the villagers poured onto the dock amid gasps of wonder and the craning of necks. Afton swayed back and forth as her body adjusted to its first time on a structure that didn't rock with the waves, or at least rocked more subtly.

Afton slowly took in the towering structures that composed the city, mouth hanging open. There was so much here that she wanted to see. The underwater greenhouses. The hatcheries. The reefs. The ocean; a wild garden that sustained the city. Her father also said that the capital had the most innovative waste reclamation system in the world, but Afton didn't feel like she needed to see that in person.

All of that would have to wait. Afton looked down at her hands, her throat going dry as she saw them trembling. She tried to retrieve her scroll, but for the first time she seemed unable to reach it. The weight of it all was an anchor on her shoulders – the reason her village had come to the city rising like floodwaters over her head. It was time to coordinate the rotations of fishing grounds, sustainability quotas, and the sharing of resources, but this year there was another issue at hand. A young girl from a small inconsequential village, just one in the vast Floating Republic, had discovered an unintended consequence of their fishing practices on the marine ecosystem. This research needed to be presented to the general assembly.

Afton clenched her fists, trying to quiet her shaking fingers. The presentation seemed so daunting. The Floating Republic was so big, and she was so small. But her father always said that a utopia was not a place where things were perfect, only a place that was willing to address its imperfections. And now she was part of that.

"Avast! Be that the great savior of our rolling seas?" The captain's booming voice rattled Afton. She turned, clenching her teeth and trying to look brave. It was a great responsibility to be the captain's daughter, and she wanted to be worthy of it. It was a great honor to be heard by the assembly. It was a privilege to be a steward of the vast maritime garden they called their home. It was all so great, and in that moment she felt so small.

The captain leaned down in front of her and took her hands in one of his, smiling with large, sympathetic eyes. With his other hand, he slowly withdrew the scroll from her belt and handed it to her. "Ready?"

Afton took a deep breath, and nodded.

Christopher R. Muscato is a writer and adjunct history professor from Colorado, USA. He is the former writer in residence of the High Plains Library District and has published nearly 2 dozen short stories, but most of his time goes to his two-year-old twins!

1 Modular approach: The entire floating village consists out of multiple smaller floating units. They are connected to each other. Each unit can be constructed separately and adapted depending on the needs. Each platform can count several levels. The modular approach makes it possible for the village to expand incrementally.

2 Tug boats: Used to tow and push the platform village. They ease maneuvering operations.

3 PSP platform: Pneumatically Stabilized Platforms

4 Monorail for maritime robots: the robot can click onto the rail and it can transport its load (mostly sea food) to the higher decks.

5 Seaweed, Kelp mariculture

6 Mussel socks

7 Small vessels used to harvest the food

8 Electric Azimuth thruster: they have a variable pitch, the angle can be changed. They are used to propel the platform and for active station-keeping.

9 Lower deck: This deck is not used for residential purposes. The deck can be overflown by (higher) incoming waves. Some equipment and technical rooms can be found here. Everything here can be anchored to the deck and can be protected against sea water. The deck can be used to deliver and ship goods.

10 Heavy equipment can be attached to the deck plate and protected with seawater proof materials. (repair parts, machines, jet skis, lifeboats, speedboats, catamarans, marine construction cranes, gantry cranes...)

11 Technical rooms, workshops, storage

12 Technical room for the drive motor from the azimuth

thruster. Designed with recycled plates from ship hulls.

13 Back-up anchor and anchor chain, used in shallow waters.

14 Elevator: it can go to just underneath sea level

15 Mbaru Niang houses

16 Protective wall

17 Searchlight

18 Fresh water pond

19 Rumah Adat, vernacular Indonesian architecture

20 Protective shield: it can be lowered down to protect the 1st residential level against bad weather

21 Sumba houses and hanging bridges

22 Town hall

23 Drinking-water reservoir

24 Platform control building: wheelhouse, chart room, radio and telecommunication room. The terraced structure is build with the Utilihab construction kit.

25 Windmills with flexible, inflated blades that can adjust their profile to the force of the wind

26 Solar panels + rain water collector

27 Primary rainwater collecting / reservoir system

28 Secondary rainwater collecting / reservoir system

29 Solar concentrator, connected to the community kitchen

30 Electricity generators

31 Drone station

32 Technical rooms for all the roof installations, made with repurposed cargo shipping containers

33 Telecom tower, radar scanners, radio mast

34 Airship & airship landing area

35 Foldable "sunflower" solar-panel field, attached on an open roof (so the rain can come through)

36 Community kitchen

37 Uma Lengge A-frame houses

38 Computer rooms

39 Drying kelp / seaweed.

40 Batak Toba house deck

41 Hanging pods

42 Vertical tubes used to grow crops

43 Food forest

44 AUV: autonomous underwater vehicle, used to monitor seaweed / kelp

---

Dustin Jacobus is a Belgian artist and industrial design engineer with special interests in biomimicry, sustainable design, and futurism. He started his career as an illustrator for the the textile industry and worked several years as a freelance designer. In 2020 he finished the art project Universitas, in which he explores a futuristic world where creativity meets science and ecology. In his latest artwork he explores how a SolarPunk future might look like. His art appeared in several international publications.
website: www.dustinjacobus.com

The Singer of Seeds

Leda Baol

Maïa climbs up the ladder and tries to sit next to me with as little noise as possible. "You're late," I mutter, and it comes out more annoyed than I am.

"I know," she whispers, crossing her legs on the sandwood boards to my mat, as she has forgotten hers again.

We stare at the landscape before us, a hand risen up to our faces, covering the left eye. Our right eye is fixed on that jagged line of mountain crests on the horizon, where the purple haze is shifting into a warm peach light.

And the sun rises.

We sit in perfect silence while the forest stretches and welcomes daylight in a concert of sounds and songs. Little steps of solitary walks populate the ground below us, chirping and tweeting messengers perform test flights in the new light of the day all around. We don't glance nor move. Although we can't see it, we feel the leaves rising all around the treehouse, the long breath of their night starting its slow release. Liquid warmth embraces our bodies when the light reaches us, entering undisturbed through the wall-high open window, reaching all angles of our one-room refuge.

It lasts no more than a couple of minutes. Then just as the new bird gathers courage and sets off the nest, the burning golden disc detaches itself from the horizon, and having assured this, we're free to go. We lower our hands.

Maïa yawns loudly over her own words. "Are you ready? D-did you sleep at all? I didn't," she stutters excitedly, "Moms say it's normal but I thought what if I don't have the energy to walk all the way to the hermitage? Do you know how far it is? It can't be that far, no?" "Give me a break. You're ten, not eighty, Maïa." I exhale, stretch my neck, turn my eyes to her. The black round spot the sun has left on my eye casts its holy shadow wherever I look. I get up, grab my bag, and begin the descent. Maïa follows, chatting happily in whispers. We get back to the Nook from behind the market, and get in line with the others who are also coming back for breakfast from the salute. Maïa runs to Mel, Deirdre and Cleo for a hug. "One day I'll figure out where you do the Hatching every day, little ones!" threatens Mel pointing at us with a smile. "Are you coming for breakfast, Elion?"

"We're going to their place," replies Maïa, grabbing my arm. "See you later!" "We'll see you at the hermitage, little ones."

Maïa gasps. "You don't come with us?"

"You're too many this year, you're going on your own," explains Deirdre. "Come on, give a kiss to mums and go." They wave goodbye to us as we leave.

"Why do you keep inviting yourself?" I complain to Maïa on the way to the cottage. "Today there's a pretty good reason, you monkey" she protests. "I want to talk with your mum again before leaving. She was a Singer too, no? Maybe she's finally going to tell us more."

"She didn't for the past two weeks you've been asking her…"

"Maybe she was waiting for today."

Dad is arranging strawberries and honey on the table outside, next to our vegetable garden. Mum is there too, picking up the rhubarb for tonight. The extra plate for Maïa is already there. Dad hugs me, scratches the short hair on my nape. "Feeling ready?"

I shrug, while Maïa is already answering on behalf of both of us. "*I* am for sure," she lies, "I don't know about Elion, they've been suspiciously silent all morning, so I think they're trying to play cool, and they're actually *terrified*."

I throw a strawberry at her face. She catches it with her mouth and winks at me, undefeated.

The bags we bring to the hermitage are empty but for the water from our homes. The group walks on steadily, with nervous but happy chatting all along the queue. We're all about the same age, two years more or two years less. The Pham twins are the youngest, seven years old. We went to school together. Their family is the only other family beside mine and Maïa's that practices the Hatching. When their little brother was born, we prayed together. I reach them. Niwa is dreamy as always, Koi is staring at the back of our guide.

The old lady walks first, following the path. Her blouse leaves her shoulders and part of her back bare. And there, her wrinkly black skin is covered in the pale pink tattoo of a blossoming peach tree.

"I want a peach tree too," murmurs Koi. "Did your mum say anything about how to get the one we want?"

"We can't."

"Of course we can't, you silly!" giggles Niwa. "There are millions of trees, plants, vegetables… What are the odds of you getting the one you feel for?"

"Well, I want something with fruit," states Koi stubbornly.

"And I'd like something that grows under the ground, in the warmth of the soil. You?" I bite my lips. I don't want to say it. "I don't know."

I don't want to say I want to go away.

The twins stop paying attention to me quite quickly. The forest is dark and deep and there's plenty to get distracted with. Our little eyes examine one by one the pulsating green life that surrounds us, wondering secretly if any of the shapes we are looking at now will one day grow on the blank of our skin.

At the edge of the flat where we come from, a big crack in the forest opens on a canyon. Down below, Beam city extends from the very narrow start of the crack up until where the canyon ends at the edge of the flat, and the desert begins. Most of us have come here already, although never by crossing the woods - it's about ten minutes with the Shinkansen, not the two hour walk we just had. We descend using wooden cabins, in groups of five. The city is beautiful from up here. And there, right in the middle of the canyon, just like a tower, the massive rock of the hermitage rises above everything else. The city woods around it gets denser, and the shining rooftops of the city become more and more rare as you get closer.

Maïa shakes me by the arm. "Can you see it?"

"Of course I can," I grumble. The hermitage is up there. Built *in* the lone rock. The caves were covered in wood and glass, with the trees that grow hanging on the sides of the rock, defying gravity with meters of void under their roots, mixing seamlessly with the construction.

While we walk in the city, people stare and smile at us. Some of them wish us good luck. A lady in dungarees points to the large green leaves covering her shoulder blades like wings and tells us she hopes to find new water lilies among us. Maïa is all proud and says hi to everyone. As we proceed towards the hermitage rock, houses are smaller and smaller, until we reach a short cobble path. "Here we go again," comments Koi next to me. He powers up the titanium implant of his right leg. We start climbing up. A sound of water comes from somewhere close. Beam city is full of streams and creeks. They come from the caves at the beginning of the valley: from there, the water runs down towards the desert and then, right before the end of the valley, it dives underground. The Waterway, they call it - mum came from there. The underground river goes on for miles and miles, feeding the towns of the people of the desert. Beam city makes sure that water is safe. And the desert towns, in partnership, sun-power the entire Beam city with their desert energy. The bamboo steps we're climbing now run all around the rock, and as we turn towards the south, there it is: the shining red dunes of my mum's homeland.

Maïa is tormenting the tip of her braid. "Will it hurt?"

Her voice is so low. She doesn't want anyone to hear.

"It doesn't. Mum said it's like a mosquito bite," I lie. "The first tattoo is so small. The ones you do after, as you grow up, take more time, but then you're already older and stronger, right?"

In truth, I didn't ask mum if it hurts. I didn't want her to know I'm scared too. Maïa sighs in relief. And in that moment, the Singer of Seeds steps in.

We gather in silence around her. She's small, and way, way younger than we all expected. She's smiling, allowing us to contemplate her tattoo. Sturdy and thick, the branches of the willow extend to her shoulders, around her neck, down to her arms until the fingertips, bright green, while her legs are covered in wrinkly roots.

"Six hundred years ago," begins the story we all know.

Six hundred years ago, after the second great collapse, the people of the flat secured all the seeds they could find in a bunker underground. While war ravaged the land, six families held onto the secret of the hermitage's location, surviving everything, sacrificing everything, for it to be found again when time was due. And only when time was due, only then, they gathered their people and shared the sacred treasure of the seeds.

And that's how humanity survived.

"You shall receive one seed," she recites. "The living being that will come from it shall be your companion for life. Wherever you'll see one, you shall be protected; whenever you'll see one, you shall protect it." Her words have begun to have music in them without us noticing exactly when. The massive gear behind her has started rotating, and the movement ignited by the sound of her voice seems to dictate the rhythm and direction of all the glass wheels within it. Thousands and thousands of tiny boxes flash indistinguishably before our eyes. "You shall return the seed you have been given before the end of your cycle under this sun, together with another one of that same species. You shall carry the seed with you, marked in your skin, growing strong just as you grow."

The players sitting at the edge of the chamber have started playing. Flutes and drums echo vigorously through the arches on top of us, all the way to the top of the opening of the cave above our heads, stronger than any sound I've heard before in my life.

"Let the song begin."

All in one, we sing. There are no words in what we're singing; or some do say something, it's not easy to understand. One by one, we step towards the Singer of Seeds, and one by one her voice tunes into ours, and just for an instant, right then, the wheel stops spinning, and quick as thunder the Singer picks the box it's stopped on, and gives it to us. There's hope in our voices; there's the vision of a planet that is ours as much as we are its own. The box in my hands has something that looks like cotton inside, and a tiny, diamond-shaped dark drop at the center of it, barely visible. Later, very soon, the Inkmaster will turn that shape into the founding point of a tattoo that one day will cover my body. And while my voice keeps singing, I daydream of islands far in the ocean, and a path that unfolds in front of me, away from everything I already know, away to places where people are not marked by seeds, where they don't welcome the Hatching of a phoenix every morning, where perhaps there's sand and underground life just like where my mother is from, or where there's ice, ice I've never seen. I daydream of the people of the mountains in the north and their trains that run on water, I see their glider highways and the ice storages on the peaks. The diggers of the steppe we receive calls from every winter, unearthing the history of our culture and rebuilding what's worth rebuilding in there before sending it out for testing all round the world, moving fast from camp to camp on the rides they choose as lifetime companions, fierce animals they have many different names for. And I see the engineers, flying from continent to continent on the helium pulsars, wiring up the technology that allows us to see all of these, and stay connected to all our loved ones everywhere, in a second.

I'll be there.

All of that, I'll see. Running after a seed that will take me to impossible places to find another alike. Exploring and mapping until my mission is complete, while my tattoo unfolds on my back as I learn, and grow, and become someone of my own.

Our song ends in a single heartbeat. We sit in perfect silence and place the box in front of us. I open mine. A little tag reads the name of my ticket to the outside world.

It's a rhubarb.

Leda Baol is a writer and designer based in Europe. She studied and worked in Italy, Scotland and the Netherlands. She enjoys investigating reality through fiction and speculative essays. In 2021, her work was published in *PostLife Mag* and the *Atticus Journal*. She is currently developing a solarpunk-themed long story. @jerichovisual / www.ledabartolucci.com

---

Tristiana

To my mother

June today, and June's days blossom one by one,
as does the rose's miraculous swirl, and its shame,
and so do cruel amoebas and enchanted beetles,
and thoughts of every crazy kind, it seems
we model summer's days from wet clay.

It seems that my mother, Cristiana, my mother, Tristia,
is already that legendary tuberose of ancient
photographs, but long a pillar of salt.
The spirits that walk our house

make the oven twitch, and it seems I am afraid
to leave this prison, afraid of someone so free,
someone like me. It seems I am closer in June
than any other to our neighbors in the solar system.

Yes, in June, I'm closer to the whole solar system
than any other, following the paper airplane
in the sky, that bird with the iron beak, accumulating
those distant lands in greed and hurry, the machine
made to save me against my uphill movement against
the downhill spin of the earth, under the moon's rheumy eyeball...

Andreea Iulia Scridon

Andreea Iulia Scridon is a poet and translator. She studied Comparative
Literature at King's College London and Creative Writing at the University of
Oxford. She has a poetry pamphlet, *Calendars*, forthcoming with Broken Sleep
Books and a poetry book, *A Romanian Poem*, forthcoming with MadHat Press
in 2022. Her debut poetry book in Romanian, *Hotare* ("Borders"), won second
place in a national manuscript contest and is published October 2021.

William of Orange

The annual trips of any schoolboy, and their circadian rhythms:
pumpkin picking in first grade,
gnome kin of those vegetables,
as squat as our legs were then.
Finally an opportunity to see the world
via its proper dimensions,
as adults are said to see it.
Yet two small beings do not make for one truth:
it's a way to walk
before we cease to be nanometric.
Lucky for us,
there's a road back,
if a tedious one.

Did Titian really love carotened women so much
as to forever bequeath them his patronymic?
Maybe every boy wants to be an artist forever,
just as the house every boy grew up in
remains the right size as he lumbers inadequate,
foot after foot,
calf after calf,
Gulliverian thigh after Gulliverian thigh –

The solar system hanging over your crib at some point
and the Red Planet in particular,
the minerals,
the manuscripts,
the paintings inside the tombs made by your unrecognizable ancestors,
the resurgence of waters onto their own shore,
the same succession of dynasties.
The threat of extinction hanging over your crib at some point,
or the possibility of life on Mars
as you watched E.T. on Sunday morning.

My parents had one child,
each and together:
absolute primogeniture,
the son of heaven, I am the eye in the sky.

The toxic hypocrisy, like McDonald's or Burger King,
of the various falsities with which to germinate the illusion of amusement:
take the color orange,
made with orpiment, lead chromate, or selenium,
or a crayon sunset you made at age eight,
crouching over the living room coffee table
with your tongue peeking diagonally out of its cage's corner;
they crucified you to the fridge.

Andreea Iulia Scridon

The Ice Moon

The orders said don't drill too deep
And stay out of the depthless ocean.
We should not disturb what is asleep
In ice. Keep frozen what is frozen.

Just bare white ice to the horizon
And screeching ceaseless winds to keep
Our imaginations in motion...
What would happen if we drilled too deep?

We programmed the drillbot's fire to keep
Its flames pressing down toward the ocean.
Ice melting down as the fires leap,
We entered the depthless ocean.

Photoluminescent explosions
Of phantasmagoria keep
Rainbows rotating in constant motion
And woke within us what was asleep.

Dreams made flesh danced for us in the deep,
So we dove deeper into the ocean
And saw all the marvels of the deep.
We didn't keep frozen what was frozen

And darkness dwelt within the ocean.
Beauty made us forget. Sudden leap
Of teeth and tentacles in motion—
An alien mouth – our final sleep—
Forgive us – We drilled too deep.

Joshua St. Claire

The Dandelions of Mars

As a boy, I must have murdered a million
and sent their severed heads skyward, snuffing
them out as a blink erases the sun.
I would grab their swollen seedheads, puffing
massive clouds that I rode up to the sky,
which showed me all the kingdoms of the world
were glittering dandelions and, flying
above, their seeds were stars. That cloud of dreams hurled
me to Mars, that great red dandelion seed.
We cheerful settlers planted the Martian dirt
with Earth's whole bounty, but nothing succeeded—
except dandelions. Just bare desert.
No more supply ships. No more seeds left. To
those dear dandelions:
                    a scream, then a whisper: *Grow!*

Joshua St. Claire

Joshua St. Claire is a married father of three boys and an accountant by trade. He enjoys writing poetry and the occasional short story when not writing financial reports. His work is published or forthcoming from Star*Line, Scifaikuest, The Flying Saucer Poetry Review, and Shoreline of Infinity, among others.

Newly cured sweet potato man

has green spouts erupting from his orange forehead.
No. He has not been too long in the sun.
More the opposite. He has been holed up, cloistered,

afraid to come out before the dark of the moon.
To appear after harvest in public with such stubble.
To stumble out. Pocked and perplexed. Short of words

and humid with doubt. He wonders who to call.
Surely a specialist. Dermatologist?
A botanist with a PhD in Morning Glories?

Or a free-range Homeopath, a traiteur, a healer,
who might open his forehead and place slices
of old onion there until they blacken with rot?

He feels uprooted. His wish for healing unheard.
The memory of Daniel Boone who died
from an overdose of sweet potatoes ripens

in his thoughts. Little solace can be found,
and less comfort in knowing his entire wardrobe,
underwear included, is not self-starching.

Richard Weaver

Richard Weaver hopes to one day once again volunteer with the Maryland
Book Bank, CityLit, the Baltimore Book Festival, and return as writer-in-residence
at the James Joyce Pub. His pubs: North American Review, crazyhorse, New
England Review, Southern Quarterly, Poetry Magazine, and Elsewhere (now
defunct). He's the author of The Stars Undone (Duende Press, 1992), and
provided the libretto for a symphony, Of Sea and Stars (2005), performed 4
times to date.
His 140th prose poem was published recently. He was one of the founders and
PE of the Black Warrior Review.

The Ambassador from the planet
formerly known as Pluto

recently paid an unexpected visit to the States
known as United. Or so it was unofficially rumored
by presidential aides who provide plausible deniability
in wholesale quantities at greater reduced reality.
These days it's clear that a dyslexic octopus has a better chance
knitting a nuclear furnace or typing Finnegan's wake
in braille, without typos, than negotiating a truce
amongst conjoined twins in love with a mongoloid banana.
And so the ambassador was engaged in double-duty-free
diplomacy to the extreme, way down to the dingle.
Without immunity, impunity, with storms raging
to the contrary, it, sexless, sans organs or urges,
rose to the occasion, and plowed a mighty furrow across
the corn crops of the mid-west, paying particular attention
to the porcine caucus in Iowa, where every oink and its echo
was counted and digitally stored, where the unique curl
of each tail was captured via CCTV and sent to storage sites
on three continents, China notwithstanding. Tariffs
be damned. What is his deep game, you may ask?
What purpose is served a la carte? Can there be shock
without awe? Or is ah & shucks enough diplomacy
for the missing masses? Five moons a circling is not enough
for the now dwarf planet? Neither is red snow.
Nitrogen glaciers and methane mountains.
Features found nowhere else in the solar system.
And now, Planet X emerges to take center stage.
Nearly Neptune in girth and stature, with a mass
10 times greater than earth, it is slow to rotate
in its elliptical orbit, if once every 15000 years can be
considered neighborly? A missing mathematical piece
of the cosmic puzzle. Allegedly. Gravitational effects
in the orbit offing of the unseen but suspected usurper planet.

Richard Weaver

Beyond the Hallowed Sky
Ken MacLeod
Orbit Books
Paperback, 368 pages, 2022
Review by Joe Gordon

I'm always happy when there is a new Ken MacLeod book to be read; for my money, he is one of the UK's most consistently impressive and thought-provoking SF writers. In *Beyond the Hallowed Sky*, we have not only a new book but the start of a trilogy – the Lightspeed series. As that would suggest, this is a story in which the development of FTL (Faster Than Light) travel is fairly prominent.

In the summer of 2067, Lakshmi Nayak receives an old-fashioned, physical letter containing detailed mathematical proofs, which would seem to indicate that FTL travel is in fact possible. It seems to echo some thoughts she has already had but not fully formulated.

But who was thinking not only on the same lines but ahead of her, and knows of her interest to contact her? Examining the letter, the seemingly impossible explanation is that she sent it to herself – from the future.

After finally publishing the work, Lakshmi's reputation is ruined by many of her peers, she eventually decides to take an offer to defect to the Union bloc and travels to Scotland, a member state. After some

Le Carré-esque spycraft in the middle of Edinburgh, the Union's AI guides her around the spies of rival powers and to a job interview on the west coast. The job offer is genuine, but the AI has other reasons, not least the development of her FTL ideas into a workable engine for a starship.

This brings us to the Clyde Coast and John Grant, a "responsible" (a person who was seriously active and important in a previous revolution in the Union), and his comrades who run an engineering co-operative making ships on the Clyde. The AI guides them together to start a collaboration that could create the first FTL ship – rather pleasingly, Clyde-built, like the great ships of the previous two centuries of tradition on that great river.

But there's more going on here. Out for a coastal stroll, John sees a submarine leaving the Faslane naval base. In this decade, Scotland is no longer part of the UK, but an independent member of the Union. However, Westminster held onto the vital nuclear submarine base of Faslane as part of the deal, and shares it with their US allies. When John sees a submarine leave the base and sail out into open water, it's nothing unusual – until it seems to hover above the waves for a moment before vanishing in a shimmering haze. Most don't believe him, and the all-seeing AI carefully wipes his photographic evidence from his devices.

Is it possible that FTL is not only viable, but other power blocs already have it?

MacLeod proceeds to gives us an expanding universe with three main arcs: our future Scotland and the small team trying to engineer their FTL ship (without the rival power blocs knowing); a Union science team on a floating base in the violent atmosphere of Venus, paying host to a visiting android who is also a spy for British Intelligence (which they are aware of – all sides are playing a version of The Great Game here); and a distant world around another star, reached by FTL, and the science teams operating there. Crossing all of this is a discovery that ties all three worlds together in a way that isn't clear yet.

The multiple, overlapping story arcs work nicely to build a three-dimensional picture of this future society, dominated by three rival power blocs. As with a number of his previous works, MacLeod conjures up a believable socio-political structure, giving it just enough details that we can grasp the situation, but not bogging it down with too much exposition, so the narrative flows at a good rate of knots. Along the way, we get to consider various weighty topics, from the notions of political ideology and patriotism to the use and limits of AI in the human sphere, and the exploration/exploitation of other worlds.

I'm Looking forward to the second volume.

My Heart is a Chainsaw
Stephen Graham Jones
Titan
496 pages, 2021
Review by Benjamin Thomas

There are countless tropes that horror fans around the world know and celebrate. Each time an unsuspecting teen or new adult dies by the blade of a masked killer seeking vengeance from an unjust act, slasher fans rejoice as the camera shot is splattered red with blood. No one more so than Jade Daniels, the high school outcast main character of Stephen Graham

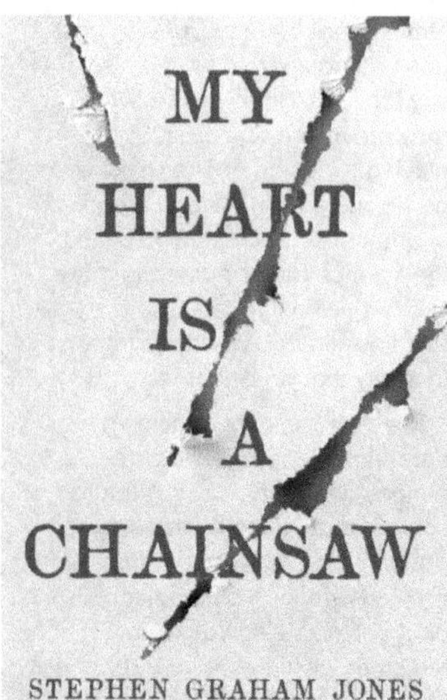

'Jones's *My Heart is a Chainsaw*.

After a teenager is found dead in an Idaho lake town, Jade is ecstatic to think that the signs are aligning, and a slasher is now walking among the citizens, ready to spark the fire of the horror movie cycle. When Jade stumbles into Letha Mondragon, her beautiful new classmate, she finds in her a flawless embodiment of a Final Girl, the one person who can take down a slasher. Through her love of horror movies, constant callbacks to the classics ('I'm looking at you *Scream*, *Texas Chainsaw Massacre*, and *Nightmare on Elm Street)*, Jade finds solace in the familiar patterns the leading ladies of these films endure. Patterns that Jade begins to see in the town around her.

However, as more bodies begin to appear, 'Jade's grip on reality begins to fray. The lines between horror movie obsession and what is real smear across one another like twin streaks of blood from the latest victims of Michael Myers.

Steeped in Native American lore and written with authenticity, *My Heart is a Chainsaw* is not only a cultural examination of our fascination with the slasher sub-genre of horror, but of how we treat our pasts and our stories, and why, sometimes, we find solace in the grotesque.

Jones paces this novel with the finesse of a top-end chef, slicing perfect strips of the rarest delicacies to 'everyone's enjoyment. His writing style conveys the 'character's emotions, as well as the importance of the setting and world around her. Peppered with term-paper extracts to further inject 'Jade's line of thinking into the novel, by the time we reach the climax, you 'can't help but stay up as late as it takes to finish the final pages and take part in an ambitious and justified ending.

While Jade's heart might be a chainsaw, nothing is more intense than the story Jones pens for her. Even if you're not a die-hard fan of horror movies or the slasher culture, this book will entertain and delight readers looking for a scary tomb of beautiful brutality. However, I'd be remiss not to add a content warning for violence, gore, abuse, suicide, and addiction.

The Cyber Puppets
Angus McAllister
Matador
paperback, 283 pages, 2018.
Review by Duncan Lunan

Angus McAllister, formerly Professor of Law at the University of the West of Scotland, has been writing science fiction for many years. His comedy SF novel *The Krugg Syndrome* was followed by the psychological thriller *The Canongate Strangler*. More recently, he has turned to murders set in Glasgow with *Close Quarters* (Matador, 2017) and *Murder in the*

Merchant City (Polygon, 2017). His prizewinning story, 'What Dreams May Come', is included in my *Starfield, Science Fiction by Scottish Writers*, reprinted by Shoreline of Infinity in 2018. For the 1995 Glasgow Worldcon he produced *Mind-Boggling Science Fiction*, a collection of his work under different pen-names, cunningly disguised as the simultaneous first and last edition of a magazine.

Those of us who've known Angus for years have always been a little bemused by his fascination with soap operas, though he did mention in MBSF that he was getting a novel out of them. I formed a thorough dislike for the genre in the sixties and after – when I couldn't avoid the ones my family insisted on watching – but in *The Cyber Puppets* Angus has avoided the banality of the British soaps and targeted the absurdities of US ones like *Dallas* and *Dynasty*.

His imagined soap follows a US-based family of Scotch whisky distillers, living in a fantasy which lets him poke fun at expatriate and would-be Scots. Don't miss the regular servings of haggis steaks, the fake Scotch whose labels "could have been printed in Disneyland", and the fake Scottish castle in which the entire family lives, complete with roof garden and swimming pool for the obligatory open-air breakfasts, and an annual party called the Highland Fling. Although it's bigger than Culzean, somehow the only rooms ever seen are the family bedrooms, the dining hall, a glimpse of the kitchen, and the library in which no one ever reads a book, like the one in the Laurence Olivier version of *Pride and Prejudice*. Likewise, their multi-storey office building has only one actual office and a boardroom. When Scott Maxwell, the family lawyer, tries to walk out, he finds that there's

an identical unused suite below, and then the stairs fade off into a void – by which time his doubts about the situation are becoming serious.

There is precedent for it: I remember a story about a soap character who became aware of the people watching him. He could see them when he turned his back on another character in order to tell him something important, as one invariably did 'out of courtesy' in his world. Angus hasn't used that particular absurdity here, but he has fun with most of the rest – like the way a girl behaves in bed as if naked, "while remembering to grab the bedclothes and hold them above her breasts, as if she suspected the presence of a hidden observer". There are signs of rebellion from the word go, as when Maxwell is deceived yet again by his unfaithful wife. "It almost seemed as if he had no control over his speech and actions... trapped inside a body that was being operated by another person... I really sound as if I mean it, he thought. I'm wasted as a lawyer. I should have been an actor." He becomes aware of the cuts from scene to scene, like the instant arrival of the police after a shooting, and a character suddenly drunk when he's only had one drink and poured another. Other characters notice the compulsion to say their lines when using the telephone, though there's nobody on the other end.

Nobody disappears without trace the way they used to do in *Compact* (the *Radio Times* once ran a letter asking when the cast of *Z-Cars* would be ordered to find them all). But Maxwell becomes increasingly aware of the cuts – how he finds himself suddenly moved from one place to another, reporting knowledge gained on the way which he has no memory of acquiring. He realises that when he looks down from his office window, there is no city below, or anything else for that matter. The last straw is when he becomes aware of the background music as he watches action he's no longer part of. His days are numbered – he's about to be written out.

But instead, like Bowman in *2001*, he finds himself in a transitional hotel-like room and being introduced to an entirely different world. The version of *The Lairds of Glendoune* in which he's been a character is not the 20th century original, but a much-enhanced 22nd-century version, computer-generated from the earlier recordings and distributed worldwide as escapism for the underground population toiling to reclaim the Earth's surface after environmental disaster – not too different from the setting of 'What Dreams May Come'. But the project has succeeded too well: the populace has become hooked on the series and is increasingly being infected with the soap's ethos of greed and dishonesty – starting with the popularity of the J.R. Ewing-type character, just as it had

in our time, but becoming an insidious threat to the very fabric of society.

Something must be done, and the attempted answer is to make the characters real and allow them to change the plots. From the outset, it hits trouble. The new synthetic people are like amnesia victims, with only partial memories of the pasts they're supposed to have had, and not all of them can break out of character to become the better rôle models which the planners were hoping for. Even worse – the new plot-lines they devise are simply not as interesting to the viewers as the old ones were.

In his 1970s contribution to the final chapter of my *Man and the Planets*, the late Chris Boyce put forward his vision of the future 'mind-machine net', and the discussion group to whom he did so spent a lot of time discussing the implications of a society in which all bodies (natural or artificial, organic or machine) were accessible to all minds.

When he returned to the subject in 1981, Chris himself had seen the dangers, remarking "the spirit of the beehive is in this". Various measures were discussed, to counter the threat to individual identity, but we didn't think of the one proposed by Socrates, the sentient computer which runs the world of *The Cyber Puppets*. 'He' proposes to jazz things up still further by giving life to a wider range of historical and fictional characters – including Moriarty, who engineered his own escape from the Holodeck in *Star Trek Next Generation*. It sounds like another bad idea, raising the possibility that Socrates, like HAL 9000, is no longer sane – but on that ominous note, the novel ends, having raised some serious issues after an enjoyable ride.

The Queen of the High Fields

Rhiannon A Grist
Luna Press
146 pages
Review by Callum McSorley

"The first time I saw the High Fields was in a dream," says The Queen of the High Fields' narrator Carys Price. This is also true for the novella's author, Rhiannon A Grist, who has turned a vision of a mythical island hidden in fog, its entrance under the sea, into a modern horror folktale which manages to feel epic in just under 150 pages.

Carys and Hazard, two teenage outcasts – Carys because she is bookish, quiet, and has the strange habit of sleepwalking into the sea, and Hazard through choice, a loudmouth punk no longer interested in anything society or even counterculture has to offer her – make a pact to reach the mythical High Fields and make it their own personal Neverland. This obsession takes years of study, eating away at their lives and friendship, and results in something which seems to be a utopia at first but inevitably goes sour.

The story flips between past and present, the dual narratives of Carys returning to the High Fields after ten years where Hazard has now become a powerful goddess and the story of how they managed to find their way there in the first place, switch with each chapter, ratcheting up the tension with each mini cliff-hanger, the pace quickening perfectly towards the finale.

The heart of story is the love between Carys and Hazard. Hazard is brash and larger-than-life, and it seems only fitting she becomes The Queen. Carys is complicated, and thorny when it comes to likability

(which works brilliantly – it makes her intriguing and you question her reliability as a narrator), torn between love, jealousy, and fear, though steely in a way that becomes more unnerving as the story progresses.

Meeting as bored teenagers stuck in a dead-end seaside town, they form an intense friendship that seems (from the distance of the reader and with a little cynicism) to last far too long, to the extent this joint goal of theirs – a pact to take the High Fields and its "Power to bend the world", in the cry of anguished teenage misfits everywhere – seems to pull each of them down as they become adults, dragging them from happiness that could have been if only they could let the High Fields, and maybe each other, go. The true cost of this power, and what they had to do to get it, comes into focus as the story progresses, expertly notching up the stakes and tension.

Grist captures this long relationship with an unfiltered eye – the intimacy, the spiky banter, the petty irritations and buried grievances, but beneath it all, the enduring love. Whether this is enough or not is left up to the reader to decide.

The ebb and flow of their partnership is reflected by the High Fields, which forms a running allegory. With the collapse of their relationship comes the collapse of the dream world they created together, putting not just themselves but the pilgrims who have come to worship Hazard in danger, giving the present-day parts of the story its urgency.

The High Fields are based on Welsh folklore, with the story of Pywll from The Mabinogion (a collection of stories compiled from oral tradition in the 12th or 13th century) in particular used as a template for Carys and Hazard's quest. The reader doesn't need any foreknowledge of this to enjoy the book as Carys's scholarly investigations into this tale in the flashback chapters provide everything you need. Through Carys, Grist deconstructs and reanalyses this centuries-old tale to provide the basis for the magic (and its rules) of her own.

Ancient epic is brought into the modern world, with swipes taken at climate change and misogynistic internet culture. The Queen gains her powers through 'witness' – a take on the trope of power gained or lost through the belief of worshippers seen in the likes of Terry Pratchett's Small Gods and Neil Gaiman's American Gods – and Carys worries exposure via the internet will remove any limit to Hazard's powers, which she is already struggling to control. It's a neat way to marry old and new and contrasts the timeless and otherworldly quality of the High Fields with the mundanity of the present nicely.

Throughout, we are treated to the weird nature of the High Fields – the complete cycle of seasons in one day and the sped-up harvest of flowers and plants, gross insects doing gross stuff, etc. – which is where Grist introduces elements of horror (via wonderfully creepy flourishes which she is brilliant at):

"The flesh of the apple was riddled with roots and leaves… The skin of each apple was slightly raised with bumps and veins from the seedling within fighting to get out. Some already had buds pushing out through the peel."

This made me squirm. There's something about taking this natural process and tweaking it in this way that makes it suddenly uncanny, unnerving, a bit disgusting, even. It's like body horror applied to plants. As odd as that may sound, it's effective. Think Annihilation by Jeff VanderMeer in its less 'out-there' moments. (That said, let's not talk about 'The Tree Scene' – all I'll say is it will stick with you for a good while afterwards.)

Grist first came to my attention through her excellent short stories (some in this magazine) and it's easy to see how she has taken the talent she developed through the short form – precise word choice, world-building in a tight space, keen sense of what scenes are necessary, what can be summarised, getting every little detail to do the maximum amount of work it can – and applied it to a longer work. What you get here is a big tale – big characters, big ideas, big themes – with the diamond-like finish of a short story.

You'll find yourself dreaming of the High Fields too.

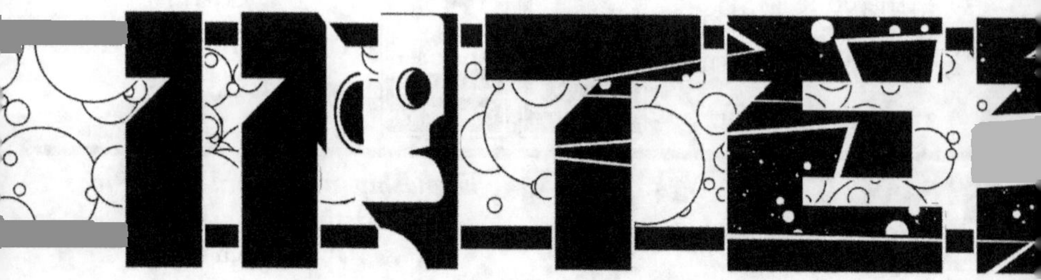

Q&A with Francesca T Barbini of Luna Press Publishing

Teika Marija Smits

asks the questions

I am delighted to talk with Francesca T Barbini of Luna Press Publishing. I've long been a fan of Francesca and the books she publishes, so it's been wonderful to get an insight into the workings of the press and how she decides which manuscripts to take on and publish – huge thanks to the ever-busy Francesca for taking the time to answer my questions.

Teika Marija Smits: *Why publishing? Or, to put it another way – if, a decade ago, you were asked the question: 'What do you see yourself doing in ten years' time?' would you have answered 'managing an independent press'?*

Photo courtesy Francesca T Barbini

Francesca T Barbini: That would be a no! Back then I was surrounded by the pieces of the puzzle, scattered all over the place. It took me a while before I was able to assemble them and see the bigger picture!

I think of myself as a facilitator; I connect people to their goals, or at least try help them along the right path. Plus, I have an entrepreneurial spirit. Couple this with my passion for writing, editing and translating, books and SFF, and this led me to Luna.

I like to experiment with new projects, work with charities, and explore the non-fiction side of SFF. Luna is *me*, so those three aspects are very important in my life as well.

TMS: *You (and your press) are based in Edinburgh, as is Shoreline of Infinity. What's the Scottish independent publishing scene like?*

FTB: I think it's a like a hidden treasure! All eyes tend to be turned towards London when it comes to publishing, but Scotland has built a very strong scene overall, and it's growing. On top of this, indie presses will always have the advantage of following their instincts and act outside of the restraints which affect the big four. This keeps the scene fresh and constantly evolving.

TMS: *Luna Press publishes in a range of genres: fantasy, science fiction, steampunk, non-fiction, Tolkien-related works, even children's books and highly illustrated books. Is there one thing that links all the books you publish, do you think? And what makes a manuscript a good fit for*

the Luna Press list?

FTB: The link, as simple as it may sound, is that the books I've published were the books that spoke to me.

I think what I consider a good fit for Luna has changed since 2015, when we started. When you read hundreds of submissions a year you become attuned to what you like and what you don't. The first thing for me is the writing style. I'm not sure I can explain this one, but I recognize it when I see it. It feels flawless, captivating, fresh, daring; it takes you straight into the story, it doesn't ask you to stop while exposition takes over – a skilled writer finds a way to tell you what has happened, *whilst* telling the story. There is also an element of subjectivity, of course, as I have to like the story itself. I don't publish "by trend", but "by heart". So, something in the content has to speak to me, for whatever reason, and at the same time it needs to feel fresh and original.

TMS: *Do you read all the submissions yourself? Or do you have a team of readers who sift through submissions? And how much of a submitter's manuscript do you actually read?*

FTB: Even when others are involved in the early stages of the submission process, I am always personally involved. We require the first three chapters of a novel, and although after all these years it takes a page or less to identify a MS you want to know more about, I make a point to reading them fully. I think three chapters is a nice amount to highlight style, flow and pace, originality.

TMS: Which brings me nicely on to my next question: You're soon to be open to novella submissions (1-2 and 8-9 of April 2022). Why should a writer submit to Luna Press?

FTB: I would turn the question around: why do you (writer) want to submit to Luna? What have you seen, or felt, when reading my blog, looking at the website, scrolling through our socials, watching our YouTube channel, that made you go, 'I'd love to be part of the Luna Family!'?

My commitment to the Luna family is there for all to see. Luna is small, but fierce, and I like to think that an author will submit to us because they have felt something, a connection, the feeling that we are the right place for their work.

(Aside from Teika: Francesca has made a brilliant series of videos about the publishing process. Do check them out!)

TMS: What has been one of your greatest challenges while running the press? And greatest successes?

FTB: Challenges: stealing the Time-Turner from Hermione Granger. Now that I can travel back and forth in time, I am able to have two full time jobs, to maintain meaningful relationships with other humans and own a beagle. Actually, the beagle owns me. Successes: Every first time we've ever had. First author signed; first book published; first review; first time seeing your books in a store; first award nomination and first win; first time selling and buying international rights; first time supplying libraries; first time working with a charity; first time working with an agent; first time watching one of our debut authors being welcomed by a much bigger publisher and the other way around. Every first time is a step forward and it fills me with excitement and joy.

TMS: How much of your week is spent working on the press? Do you have a team about you?

FTB: Every day, including weekends! I guess when you are a small business owner it's harder to switch off. I have become better at planning "me time", but I can still improve on that! I run Luna by myself primarily, but there are awesome freelancers who help me out and others who take care of certain aspects of the production process. I couldn't do it without them.

TMS: *Any hard-won wisdom (about life or publishing!) that you'd like to pass on?*

FTB: When your heart and soul are in a project, it will never feel like a chore. The moment you lose that drive, be honest to yourself, reassess and get back to the drawing board.

Running a small press is really hard, so when I feel overwhelmed, I stop and take 'my pulse'. As long as the flame is still burning, I can rally and carry on. I need to give 100% to my authors, so my commitment needs to be unfaltering.

TMS: *As a former publisher myself (and now editor-at-large) I know it's hard to single out any one title as being a 'favourite', but if there is one Luna Press book that we should all go out and buy right now, what would it be?*

FTB: We have three novels lined up for this year, John Dodd's debut science fantasy *Ocean of Stars*, Cat Hellisen's retelling of Snow White from the point of view of the step-mother, *Cast Long Shadows* [Ed: We publish the first chapter in this issue of Shoreline to give you a taste], and Lorraine Wilson's *The Way the Light Bends*, a dark fantasy story set in Scotland. I am very excited about these books. And yes, I know that I have given you three titles... I cannot pick !

TMS: *Lastly... tea or cappuccino, a Bellini or Chianti...?!*

FTB: Cappuccino and Bellini sounds good to me! But Chianti with my meals (with or without the fava beans).

Luna Press Publishing is at www.lunapresspublishing.com where you will find links to Luna's Twitter account and Youtube channel.

This interview was first published online at www.thebookstewards.com Shoreline of Infinity is grateful to The Book Stewards for giving permission to publish it here.

MILK, by our cover artist Stref, published by Shoreline of Infinity

"MILK contains some of the most beautiful, expressive art that I've seen in a long time. It deserves to be a huge commercial success."

—Alan Grant

Shoreline of Infinity is based in Edinburgh, Scotland, and began life in 2015.

Shoreline of Infinity Science Fiction Magazine is a print and digital magazine published quarterly in PDF, ePub and Kindle formats. It features new short stories, poetry, art, reviews and articles.

But there's more – we run regular live science fiction events called Event Horizon, with a whole mix of science fiction related entertainments such as story and poetry readings, author talks, music, drama, short films – we've even had sword fighting.

We also publish a range of science fiction related books; take a look at our collection at the Shoreline Shop. You can also pick up back copies of all of our issues.Details on our website...

www.shorelineofinfinity.com

www.ingramcontent.com/pod-product-compliance
Lightning Source LLC
Chambersburg PA
CBHW070405200726
48294CB00003B/1104